PRAISE FOR

MYSTERIES:

"...the book is enriched by the author's cleverly phrased prose and convincing characterization. The surprise ending will satisfy and delight many mystery fans. A diverting mystery that offers laughs and chills." -*Kirkus Reviews*

"An impressive cozy mystery from a promising author." -*Mystery Tribune*

"A really funny mystery with a chicklit feel." -Susan M. Boyer, USA Today Bestselling Author of *Lowcountry Bordello*

"Designer Dirty Laundry shows that even the toughest crime is no match for a sleuth in fishnet stockings who knows her way around the designer department. A delightful debut." -Kris Neri, Lefty Award-Nominated author of *Revenge For Old Times' Sake*

"Combining fashion and fatalities, Diane Vallere pens a winning debut mystery...a sleek and stylish read." -Ellen Byerrum, National Bestselling author of the Crime of Fashion mysteries

"Vallere once again brings her knowledgeable fashion skills to the forefront, along with comedy, mystery, and a saucy romance. *Buyer, Beware* did not disappoint!" -*Chick Lit Plus*

"Fashion is always at the forefront, but never at the cost of excellent writing, humorous dialogue, or a compelling story." -*Kings River Life*

"A captivating new mystery voice, Vallere has stitched together haute couture and murder in a stylish mystery. Dirty Laundry has never been so engrossing!" -Krista Davis, *New York Times* Bestselling Author of The Domestic Diva Mysteries

"Samantha Kidd is an engaging amateur sleuth." -*Mysterious Reviews*

"It keeps you at the edge of your seat. I love the description of clothes in this book...if you love fashion, pick this up!" -*Los Angeles Mamma Blog*

"Diane Vallere takes the reader through this cozy mystery with her signature wit and humor." -Mary Marks, *NY Journal of Books*

"...be careful; you might just laugh right out loud as you read." -3 no 7 Looks at Books

STARK

A SAMANTHA KIDD MYSTERY

RAVING

MOD

STARK RAVING MOD

Book 13 in the Samantha Kidd Mystery Series

A Polyester Press Mystery

This is a work of fiction. Characters, places, and events are the product of the author's imagination or are used fictitiously. Any resemblance to real people, companies, institutions, organizations, or incidents is entirely coincidental.

e-ISBN: 9781954579378

paperback ISBN: 9781954579415

❦ Created with Vellum

STARK

A SAMANTHA KIDD MYSTERY

RAVING

MOD

DIANE VALLERE

Polyester Press

To Gigi, Lisa, and Ellen. Long live the FF!

1

APRIL MAY

THERE'S NOTHING QUITE AS EXCITING AS A PADLOCKED trunk. At least on a Tuesday afternoon, in the middle of a dry news spell, when all of the donuts had been eaten and it wasn't yet time for happy hour. Newsrooms can be boring, so the arrival of my trunk was of interest to everyone.

"What's inside?" Carl Collins asked. Carl was the resident expert on all things Ribbon—as in Ribbon, Pennsylvania, the town where we lived. He covered homicides, obituaries, and stories of local interest. He dressed like Kolchak the Night Stalker: seersucker suit and Stan Smith sneakers, explaining his choice both as a nod to a beloved character and a way to free his mind from thinking about clothes. In a way, he was the complete opposite of me.

My name is Samantha Kidd. I'm an occasional style columnist for the local newspaper which I am uniquely qualified for thanks to a decade working for an upscale retailer in New York before giving it all up to move back to Ribbon. Sometimes I help the police solve crimes (though they don't always classify what I do as "help"). I'm probably not uniquely qualified for that, but I like to think I bring something special to the table.

In addition to my style column, my editor tasked me to write a special feature called "Untying the Mysteries of Ribbon." I had a knack for sniffing out mysteries in our small town, and this was his way of getting me to use my powers for good and not evil. Or more precisely, for circulation.

The mystery of Ribbon that I was about to untie was a sealed trunk I bought at auction. It was from the estate of Boyd Brighton, the lead singer of the Modifiers, a British band who'd had success with a string of hit singles in the sixties. The band had remained relevant for the early part of the decade, but parked their Lambrettas for good in 1965 right around the time Dylan plugged in. The band's first (and only, it turned out) album had risen through the charts and was a natural for a follow-up. But after the clash between the Mods and Rockers on the Whitsun bank holiday in Brighton, England in 1964, to the dismay of his label, Boyd quit the band and dropped out of sight.

If it seems odd to you that the estate of a reclusive English pop star from the sixties ended up in Ribbon, Pennsylvania, then you're not alone. Unbeknownst to most followers of the band, and it turns out there were many, Boyd died without a will. Thanks to something called Bona Vacantia, his unclaimed estate became the property of the English government. After he died, it remained with them for thirty years and was donated to a charity who raised more money by making the lot available to a network of auction houses than selling it off piecemeal in a retail store. Harrington's Auction House won the bid and the lot of Boyd Brighton memorabilia traveled from England to Pennsylvania not long after.

The main attraction of the auction was Boyd's music memorabilia and equipment. Those items were estimated to bring in four to five figures each. The glossy auction catalog contained page after page describing vintage musical equipment that had been both on tour and in the studio with the band, and collectors were expected to turn out en masse. But unlike the equipment, with well-documented authenticity thanks to publicity stills and concert footage, there was nothing to prove the trunk ever belonged to Boyd so it was a footnote to the rest of the auction, and I bought it for the low price of fifty bucks. Hello, discount shoppers. I am your leader.

"Do you have a key?" Carl asked

"It didn't come with a key," I said. "That's part of the mystery."

While the rest of us hovered around the trunk, one of the interns set a pair of bolt cutters on my desk. "I borrowed these from maintenance," he said. "José wants them back by five."

Mystery trunk: check. Bolt cutters to cut off the padlock: check. Strength to use the bolt cutters:

questionable. Exercise to me meant doing bicep curls with a slice of pizza.

In anticipation of opening a sealed trunk from the sixties, I'd channeled my inner *That Girl* and dressed in a cobalt blue shift dress, red tights, and white boots and styled my somewhat curly almost black hair into a flip. A few months ago, I donated twenty-five bags of clothes to a shelter in an effort to let go of my baggage. No one warns you that divesting yourself of your wardrobe has the inverse effect of creating a need for clothes. I now shopped based on whatever was happening in my life at the time, and what was happening now was mod.

"Yo, Kidd!" my editor bellowed across the bullpen. "My office. Now."

I set the bolt cutters down. I left the group huddled around the trunk. Monty had been a part of the paper since they typeset the thing, and when he barked your name, you jumped.

"What's up?"

"There's a man here to see April May," Monty said. "I told him she worked for you. Can you handle him?"

"Sure," I said.

It would have been nice to have an assistant working for me, but the truth was April May was my alter ego. When "Untying the Mysteries of Ribbon" launched, it came with a pseudonym, something about diversifying the by-lines and keeping the name Samantha Kidd synonymous with style. I didn't put up an argument; it seemed foolish to undermine my fashion column, and pretty soon every article in the paper (except for sports) would be by me or Carl. I wasn't accomplished enough of a journalist for that kind of credit. Monty let me pick a name. I picked April May. It was easy to remember and easy to forget which fit the bill on any possible motivation I would need.

"He's waiting by the doors."

A blond man in an olive green fishtail parka worn over a narrow suit jacket and crisp Levi 501s with a two inch cuff and stood by the entrance to the paper. His jeans were cuffed above his ankles, exposing redline selvedge denim and argyle socks that peeked out above black penny loafers.

I left my coworkers waiting by the trunk and approached him. "Hi," I said. "I'm April. You wanted to see me?"

"Ronnie Holiday," he said. "Is there a place we can talk?"

"Follow me."

I led him to the conference room. As conference rooms went, it was average. A long wooden table sat in the middle, surrounded with chairs purchased in bulk at the local office supply store. A bookcase filled with bound issues of the *Ribbon Eagle* from the past fifty years took up the wall to the left, and a framed picture from the year the paper launched hung on the right. Directly in front of me was a wall of windows, covered in blinds that were partially open, allowing thin horizontal strips of light to trickle in.

"How can I help you, Mr. Holiday? I asked.

"I want the trunk," he said. There was an edge to his voice, something between demanding and desperate.

"What trunk?" I asked even though the question made me appear obtuse.

"The trunk from the Boyd Brighton auction." He leaned in closer. His breath smelled sour. "You have it, right?"

I leaned back to put distance between Ronnie's breath and my nose. "May I ask why you're interested in it?"

Ronnie hesitated for a moment too long, and I knew whatever he was going to say was going to be a lie. "I'm a collector," he said finally. "I'm interested in mod and mod revival memorabilia."

"Nobody knows if anything in the trunk fits the description," I said.

"You haven't opened it?"

"We were about —" I stopped speaking abruptly. I sometimes had to elaborate on the truth to make a story seem interesting. I didn't know what was in the trunk, and I didn't want Ronnie to be there when I found out. It was possible I'd paid fifty dollars for a trunk filled with guitar strings and socks that smelled like his breath, but that's the risk I had to take. "Give me your number," I said. "I bought the trunk for an article, but when I'm done going through it, I can sell it to you."

"No," he said definitively. His fist pounded on the conference room table to emphasize the point. "I need first access." he added. He pulled out a slip of paper and handed it to me.

I unfolded it. "You're offering me $50,000 for a trunk that cost me fifty bucks?"

"Don't toy with me, Lady. It won't turn out well for you."

It was entirely possible that the mystery of Ribbon I was about to untie was why someone would pay me fifty grand for a sixty-year-old sealed trunk, and if I were a reporter like Carl, I may have saved time solving that mystery instead. But I wanted to know what was in the trunk. I wanted to know why the stranger who wandered into the newspaper wanted to buy it out from under me. I wanted to know how he knew I worked here, and how he knew I was the trunk owner.

That was a good question.

"How did you find me?"

"The auction keeps records of buyers."

"I thought those records were confidential."

"I want the trunk, Miss May," he said. "I can be very persistent." He pulled out a business card and tossed it on the conference table. "If you know what's good for you, you won't waste my time." He turned around and stormed out of the building.

2

AVOCADO TOAST AND LAVENDER
TEA

I picked up his business card. "Ronnie Holiday,"
It read. "Creative Director of The Mod Holiday"
followed by an address and website. I knew the location;
it was next to one of my new favorite restaurants. I
flipped the card over. The back said: ~~London~~, ~~Paris~~, ~~Milan~~,
Ribbon. The first three cities had lines drawn through
them. I rubbed my thumb over the words only to
discover the strikethrough lines were part of the design.
Someone had a sense of humor.

I approached the window to the conference room
and peeked out from between the blinds. The *Ribbon
Eagle* building was only two stories high, so it wasn't
difficult to make out Ronnie exiting the building or
watching him walk to a dark blue Lexus. Moments later,
he pulled out exited the lot.

The excitement of my trunk had dissipated and my
coworkers—Carl, Monty, and a handful of editors and
part-time interns—had returned to their stations. My

trunk remained where I'd left it, in the middle of my desk in my cubicle. The open lock dangled from the trunk, and the bolt cutters were gone. A piece of clear tape that wouldn't deter anybody from anything held the trunk shut.

"Who took off the lock?" I asked Kristi, the blonde in the cubicle next to me. She was a sweet twenty-three year old recent college graduate who wore dresses with tiny flowers and sneakers with giant soles. Kristi ran the paper's social media accounts. After a brief stint as an influencer, I'd decided I wanted as little to do with social media as I could, so I went out of my way to keep Kristi happy. That usually involved avocado toast and lavender tea.

"José needed his bolt cutters back," she said. "Monty told him to cut the lock before he took them, but he put the tape on so you'd still be the first one to look inside.

"Kidd!" Monty bellowed. Despite a penchant for cigars and about a hundred extra pounds of weight hanging around his midsection, the man could yell. I looked across the bullpen and he pointed inside his office. It was that kind of day.

"Don't let anybody else touch it," I said to Kristi.

I went to Monty's office. "Close the door," he said. I eased the door shut. "What did that man want?"

"The trunk. He offered me fifty thousand dollars for it."

Monty's face clouded and his mouth turned down. "How much did you pay?"

"Fifty bucks."

Monty didn't seem nearly as surprised as I was. "What do you know about it?"

"About as much as they wrote in the auction catalog. It came from the Boyd Brighton estate, but there's no proof it had anything to do with Boyd. It's been sealed for over fifty years." Just saying it caused my fingers and toes to tingle.

"Did you take photos at the auction?"

"They didn't allow cameras. I tried to shoot from the hip, but all I got were shoes."

Monty nodded again. He picked up a stack of pink message slips from his desk and waved them at me. "I've gotten four offers to buy that trunk since this morning. You sure no one saw the contents at the auction?"

"That's what the program said."

Monty appeared to be conflicted. A story about a sealed trunk might get likes on our Facebook page, but it wasn't going to move papers. The fifty dollars I'd taken from petty cash to pay for the trunk had put a dent in our monthly donut budget, but for fifty grand we could buy ourselves a donut franchise. Not that we would, but it's good to have options.

Monty turned around and stared out the window. "Why would somebody pay that much for a sealed trunk?" he asked.

"He said he's a collector."

"Collectors are a special breed."

"I don't think he was a collector," I said. I pulled out Ronnie's card and flapped it back and forth. "He owns a store called The Mod Holiday. He got the name April

May from the auction house and traced her here. We've kept her identity under lock and key since she started writing for the paper. It shouldn't have been that easy for him to ferret her out."

Monty took the card and stared at it. "The Mod Holiday," he repeated. "Cute," he added, almost absentmindedly. I could think of twenty cuter names for a mod store if given five minutes and a pot of coffee, but it didn't seem this was a brainstorming session.

If Monty wanted to send a message to the employees of the paper, he'd leave his door open so everybody could hear our conversation. There were only two reasons he'd call me into his office and shut the door and neither had to do making an example out of me. One was to talk about April May's stories without letting anyone else hear. The other was to discuss confidential newspaper business. I'd like to say the latter was because he respected my business acumen, but it had more to do with the fact that, for the most part, I funded my stories.

A little over a year ago, an anonymous source awarded me a sizeable chunk of change as a thank you for exposing corruption in our small town. For the first time in my life, I chose not to handle it myself, and my skilled financial advisor parlayed the money into a tidy little nest egg. He encouraged me to find worthwhile investments, I told him I liked shoes, and Nick told me no way. I continued to keep an eye out for investment possibilities, but in the meantime, I spread the wealth.

"Fifty grand is a lot of money," I said quietly. "Do you

want me to sell?" Monty remained at his window a moment longer.

After a long pause, he turned. "Call him back."

I understood exactly what Monty was saying. The *Ribbon Eagle* was a hundred and fifty-year-old, privately-owned paper, and local newspapers were a novelty. The *Philadelphia Post* ran the same national stories that we did and I doubted their contributors went by fake names to flesh out their by-lines. I wasn't a fan of the *Post*, none of us were, but we were in a newspaper war. It was like the Jets versus the Sharks with pencils instead of switchblades—or at least it might have been if we didn't type out our stories on keyboards.

I never expected my life's work to involve the local paper. My passion was fashion. Writing about trends was a way to stay connected to the fashion industry. At first, I contributed an occasional style column. In time, I shifted my focus from what others were wearing to why they were wearing it. My article on hemlines as an indicator of economic stability got seventeen fan letters, a *Ribbon Eagle* record. Plus, I had a cubicle and everything.

I left Monty's office and found Kristi inserting sparklers into a tray of cupcakes.

"We're about to celebrate the paper's anniversary," she said. "Aren't you coming?"

"I'll join you in a minute."

I headed back to my desk to get to work on my assignment, but even though José had cut the lock off the trunk, a new problem prevented me from accessing the contents.

Specifically, the trunk was gone.

3

ANTICLIMACTIC

"Where's the trunk?" I asked everyone and no one in general. I looked around. The bullpen was empty. I turned in a slow circle and heard my colleagues in the conference room. Kristi carried her tray of cupcakes into the room and the noise level increased. I went to the door.

"Hey!" I called. Oswald, one of our newer interns, looked at me. Oswald was a twenty-year-old who wore bowties with short sleeved dress shirts and coordinated suspenders that he clipped onto his jeans. "What happened to the trunk?" I asked.

"That guy took it down to your car," he said.

"What guy?"

"I don't know what guy. I assumed you asked him to help you. Why?"

Interns!

I raced out of the room to the window. A tall man in a black denim jacket and covered in band patches and skinny jeans had his arms wrapped around my trunk. I left the window and raced down two flights of stairs to the parking lot then burst out the doors. "Hey!" I shouted. "That's mine!"

The man glanced over his shoulder and dropped the trunk. It opened on impact. Colorful garments in paisley, plaid, and floral spilled out with more classic shades of navy, red, and white. The man took off on foot and rounded the corner where I lost sight of him. I'm not the sort to wear footwear appropriate for a street chase, so I let him get away and went to the spilled trunk contents.

The trunk sat on its side. I righted it. I folded a color-blocked dress, knocked off from Yves St. Laurent's famous Mondrian collection, and set it inside, then added a blue and purple paisley jacket, several corduroy miniskirts, a stack of men's trousers. A knot of neckties and cravats were bound together with a piece of string. Two short white boots, a pair of penny loafers, and a wad of colorful tights now stuck to the rough macadam were the last of it, until I spied a cigar box bound with a rubber band a few feet away.

As far as unboxings went, it was anticlimactic.

I corralled the mess into the trunk, then shut the lid and closed the hatch. My car was two rows over, but my keys were inside the building. The trunk was too heavy to carry, so I grabbed the handle on the side and dragged it behind me to the elevator in the lobby.

When I returned to the newspaper offices, the party

was still in swing. I pulled Ronnie Holiday's card from my pocket and called him.

"This is April May from the *Ribbon Eagle*," I said. "I've reconsidered your offer to buy the trunk."

"Are the contents intact?" he asked. His voice held a tinge of desperation.

"I don't know," I said honestly. I hadn't had a chance to examine the contents myself, so I had no way of knowing if anything was missing. "I think so," I added.

"I'm on my way back to you." He disconnected.

I wasn't entirely happy about Ronnie returning to the paper, but this was a somewhat public location, and I wasn't alone. Carl had taken to working late hours sometimes well into the night, and Monty practically lived here. But I couldn't help wondering about the attempted theft of the trunk and whether or not it was a good idea to draw more attention to the paper.

I went back to Monty's office and poked my head in the door. "Ronnie Holiday is on his way," I said. "You don't happen to know where I could get a padlock do you? He thinks I haven't opened the trunk and if it's locked, he won't ask questions."

Monty turned around and spun the dial on a lock on the file cabinet behind him. He removed the lock and held it out to me. "Take this. The combination is sixty-four, eighteen, five."

"Thanks." I spun the lock in a circle, then looked back up at Monty. "You said you've had four offers to buy the trunk?" Monty nodded once and tapped his fat, calloused index finger on the pink messages on his desk. "So far today I've had one offer to buy the trunk and one attempt to steal it." I waited a few seconds to give Monty a chance to respond. He was a newspaper editor—he'd been the newspaper editor for decades—and he appeared to either be in it for the news or the chance to yell at people. (I gave him the benefit of the doubt.) I finally added, "Are you sure you want me to sell? It seems there might be a story there."

Monty made a notation on his paper calendar. "There is no story. Sell the trunk."

"I'll handle it."

As I made my way back to my desk I rounded the corner to my cubicle. The trunk was open and the contents covered my blotter. A red plastic Solo cup rested on a blue napkin. Kristy held her phone up and her flash went off.

"What are you doing?"

"I'm taking pictures for the blog."

"You can't — it's not — I'm not doing this story."

"Why not?"

"I'm selling the trunk"

"But Monty said —"

"Monty changed his mind."

For the second time, I scooped up the contents, knocking the red cup over in the process. Fizzy liquid spilled onto my desk blotter. I dropped the clothes into the trunk, grabbed the papers and shook them off, then wiped them off as best as I could with the blue napkin. "What was that?" I asked.

"Champagne. You didn't come to the party, so I brought the party to you."

I pulled my desk drawer open and tossed the damp pages and book on top of Ronnie's business card. I closed the trunk. "Remember the man who was here earlier?" I asked Kristi.

Kristi shook her head. "I was busy with the party decorations."

"Right before José cut the lock off the trunk. A man came in and asked for April."

"I haven't met April yet."

"That's not important." I tamped the pile of clothes down so they fit into the trunk and wedged the cigar box into the side. I tried not to focus on the contents too closely, but it was impossible not to wonder about the garments inside. I turned my head away from the trunk so I wouldn't get too attached.

Fifty dollars. Unbelievable.

"A man is coming to buy the trunk, and he thinks it's never been opened." I fed Monty's lock through the hasp. "You can either stay here and lie with me, or you can go back to the party and pretend this never happened."

"I'm a terrible liar," she said.

I picked up the now-empty cup and handed it to her. "Go have fun."

After Kristi left, I removed the lock, grabbed the cigar box, and slipped it into my desk drawer. Who would know? I closed the trunk, snapped Monty's lock into place, and used a dry corner from the blue napkin to wipe off remaining droplets of champagne. I pulled the desk blotter out from under the trunk, bent it in half, and jammed it into my trash bin, then carried the bin to the hallway. The elevator doors opened, and I looked up, expecting to see Ronnie.

Two men dressed in head to toe black got out. They each carried a small white Styrofoam cooler. The taller of the two pushed me out of the way and entered the newspaper office.

I regained my balance and ran after them. "Hey!"

The tall man turned and aimed his flashlight at me. The shorter man pulled two plastic bottles of water out of his pockets and dumped them into the coolers. Thick white smoke billowed out of the top and made it difficult for me to see. I didn't know what they were doing, so I pulled my collar up over my mouth and breathed through it.

"The trunk," the taller man growled. He either had the deepest voice I'd ever heard, or he was wearing a voice distorter.

"It's here," his partner said. The man turned away from me and ran toward my cubicle. Their flashlight beams bounced around the white fog, indicating where they were. The party was probably raging inside the closed conference room, and as much as I wanted to join my coworkers, I desperately hoped nobody would get the idea to come find me. I crept toward the closest cubicle and slowly dropped down to my knees. My throat was dry and I could barely speak.

A red Solo cup, like the one I knocked over at my

desk, sat at Carl's workstation. I picked it up and chugged. It was champagne. Bubbles coated my throat but left my arms feeling thick and heavy. I got to my feet and peered over the top of the cubicle. The men each grabbed a handle of the trunk and headed toward the elevator.

Monty's door opened and he looked out. He waved his hand back and forth, and I could see the smoke, thickest by the center of the bullpen, curling into tendrils around him.

I hiccupped. The shorter man dropped the trunk. It was an unexpected distraction. The man whirled toward me, and the one in front grabbed his arm and pulled him forward.

"Let's go," he said. They abandoned the trunk and ran out of the building.

4

APRIL FOOL

"What's going on out here?" Monty asked.

"Don't come too close," I called, then hiccupped again. "They released a knock-out gas."

I held my breath to get the hiccupping under control and tried to breathe. The air felt cool. I opened a window and then joined Monty by desk. Smoke billowed out of the two coolers. Monty jabbed at it with a pencil. "Dry ice," he said. "Like at a Halloween party. Was that one of Carl's 'April is a Fool' jokes?"

Only three people at the paper knew I was April May: me, Monty, and Carl. I would have liked to keep it between me and my editor, but Carl got anxious when a new reporter started getting by-lines and demanded to see April's qualifications. Monty let it slip that I was her reference, and Carl badgered me until I caved. (Since then, I've been reading articles about how to hold up under interrogation.) And since then, Carl set out to turn every day into April Is a Fool Day and made it his mission to make me the fool.

I stared inside the cooler, and then looked toward the elevator. What had happened? Two men in black dropped off coolers of dry ice and attempted to steal my trunk. Monty picked something up from the floor. It was a black plastic water gun with a flashlight taped to the top. "It's a toy," I said.

"Gotcha, Kidd," Carl called out across the bullpen. He approached with two red cups in his hands. "April fool," he said when no one else was in earshot. He extended a cup toward me. I took it and threw the contents on him in response. My aim was exceptional; from my seated position, I managed to cover the front of his pants.

"That's enough," Monty barked. "I don't want to hear about another one of these practical jokes. You two got that?"

"Got it," Carl said. He pretended to look sheepish, but as soon as Monty was back in his office, he grinned again. "You should have seen the look on your face. Oh, wait! You can. I had Kristi set up her camera to film the whole thing." He went to Kristi's desk and removed a cell phone from a tripod. He tapped the screen a few times. "I can't wait to print up Christmas cards this year."

It wasn't the day to sit around being a punchline. My husband, shoe and sneaker designer Nick Taylor, was leaving for a shoe show in Italy tomorrow, and we maintained a tradition of dining out the night before his trips.

I called Nick. "Hi," I said. "Are you all packed?" I asked.

"I've been packed since noon," he said. The tense edge that had become present in Nick's voice was gone. "I haven't looked forward to a work trip like this for years. It finally feels like things are moving forward. Are we still on for dinner?"

"Absolutely." I fingered Ronnie's card. "How do you feel about fusion?"

"If you're thinking The Pho, then I'm in."

"Great minds. I'll meet you there in twenty minutes." I hung up and turned to Monty. "Time for me to leave. That man is coming back to buy the trunk. Don't you think it's wise to have Carl babysit it until he shows up?"

Monty agreed. "Party's over, Collins. Kidd, get out of here before I change my mind."

Carl grumbled but planted himself in my seat. This time it was my turn to grin. "Have a nice night," I sing-songed. "I'll expect my money when I get back in the morning." I grabbed my handbag and left.

I arrived at The Pho, an Irish-Asian fusion restaurant that combined Celtic food with the traditional Vietnamese noodle house. The owners, Phil Kim and Petra Moon, were a sixty-year-old couple who lived in the same apartment building as Nick's dad. The place could have been a joke if the owners didn't share a passion for cooking. Phil was a regular at Nick's dad's weekly poker game, and it wasn't unusual for him to cash out with gift cards. Nick Senior was more of a pizza-and-Peroni man, so the gift cards often came to us.

Behind me, a parade of motorcycles turned into the lot of the Kirkville Hotel across the street. As businesses came and went from Ribbon, interesting juxtapositions emerged. This intersection was no exception. The Pho had a mod theme, counter to the rough-and-tumble atmosphere of the biker bar across the street. I was less interested in things that contrasted than things that went together; Ronnie Holidays' shop was right next door.

Nick was waiting out front of the restaurant. His curly brown hair, now shot through with enough silvery threads to give him that distinguished-but-still-sexy older man vibe that George Clooney had in the Ocean's movies, was rumpled, and his white broadcloth shirt looked like he'd slept in it. Since launching Saint Nick, his designer sneaker collection, sleep-deprived Nick was more common than not, but the twinkle in his root-beer-barrel-colored eyes sparkled with the anticipation of his upcoming trip to Italy.

After some professional trouble, Nick finally managed to sign Blak Friiday, a former defensive linebacker for the Eagles who retired and launched a secondary career in Hip Hop, to be the face of his brand. Blak's retirement wasn't completely by choice; an undiagnosed broken foot had led to chronic pain that led to a rapidly deteriorating performance on the field. What his fans didn't know was he suffered from plantar fasciitis which made him a self-taught expert on shoes.

When Nick reached out to him to talk about a collaboration, Blak said hella yeah, and now the two were thick as thieves. Nick claimed he needed a break from traveling, but I had a feeling a trip to Italy with a Super Bowl winner-turned-rapper wouldn't be too miserable.

We kissed hello. I glanced behind us and saw a crowd of men in black leather jackets loitering by their motorcycles. One man stared back at me. I turned away and followed Nick inside, then turned back when I realized why he looked familiar: he looked like the man who tried to carry the trunk out of the newspaper offices. I tried to shake the feeling that I was being watched, but when Nick chose a table by the window, I shook my head and pointed one in the back.

The interior of the restaurant was decorated in graphic black and white: checkerboard floor, white tables, black placemats, white bowls, black chopsticks. One could argue it was modeled after a pair of Vans black and white checkered sneakers, and one might be correct, because the job had been done by my best friend, Eddie. I might not have remembered if he hadn't walked up that that moment.

"Hey, Dude," Eddie said. He pulled up a chair, flipped it around and straddled it.

Eddie Adams was my best friend and the person I'd call if I ever needed to move a body. Eddie is mostly agreeable, except during the holidays, because he works in the field of visual merchandising. We went to high school together, lost touch for close to a decade, then reconnected over a murder (as lifelong friends sometimes do). These days he worked freelance for the city of Ribbon, installing displays to promote whatever seasonal events the mayor dreamed up. It was well-paying work that kept him dressed in message tees, paint-stained cargo pants, and black and white checkered Vans, just the way he wanted life to be.

"Not willing to chance it with her cooking tonight?" he asked Nick.

I glanced back and forth between Nick and Eddie's faces. It was true I wasn't known for my culinary abilities but learning to cook seemed a worthwhile pursuit and now I burned dinner three times a week. In unrelated news, my favorite pizza place reported an increase in business on corresponding dates. I'm almost certain that's a coincidence.

"What are you doing here?" I asked Eddie. "I thought you finished this job."

"I did. There's a new store moving in next door, and I'm scoping them out."

"The Mod Holiday?"

"You've heard of it?" Eddie asked.

"The owner came into the paper today.

"Petra said they wanted to hire me."

"Is that a good thing or a bad thing?"

"It's an I-don't-know thing. That's why I'm here."

Eddie ran his palms over his recently buzzed head. On any given day, Eddie could be found wearing a mohawk, a shaved head, or long, floppy blond hair. He changed his hair the way most people changed their shoes, but in Eddie's case, his shoe choice was ridiculously consistent. The only time I'd seen him not wearing black and white checkered Vans was either due to inclement weather or a need to be stealthy, which, come to think of it, happened more than you'd think.

This recent hairstyle change came as a convenience. He'd let his hair grow to shoulder length, and twice in the past month it had gotten it caught in the rig of a visual installation on Penn Avenue. There's something about accidentally gluing your hair to a light fixture that makes a person question their personal grooming choices. Out came the clippers, off went the hair, and now women and children crossed the street when they saw him riding his skateboard toward them.

"So you're taking off for Italy tomorrow?" Eddie asked Nick.

"Yep. I'll only be gone four days. Can you keep her out of trouble until I get back?"

"Dude," Eddie said. "I'm only human." Eddie stood and turned his chair back around. "I gotta split." He swiped a piece of phoda bread—soda bread made with a pho cube—from our basket and left.

I watched Eddie through the window. As he drove away in his VW bug, a dark blue Lexus slowly followed. Eddie turned left and the Lexus went straight and drove past the bikers loitering in front of the bar across the street. It was the second time today I'd seen that same car. What was Ronnie Holiday doing here? Was he following me?

"Kidd? What's wrong?" Nick asked.

I pointed to the window. "I know that guy. He came to the paper today." I excused myself from the table and went out front. My first phone call was to Carl. "Did Ronnie Holiday come back and get the trunk?" I asked.

"Yeah. He was mad. He's going to call you."

"He doesn't have my number."

"He does now. He gave you fifty thousand dollars. I thought he earned it. Besides it's not like it's unlisted."

"Thanks for nothing, Collins." I hung up.

The blue Lexus disappeared around the back of the Kirkville hotel, and I lost sight of it. The tallest of the bikers followed and it was then that I remembered where I'd seen him before. He was the man who tried to steal the trunk earlier today. Maybe they were working together. Or more likely, Carl's stunt had left me suspicious of everyone's behavior.

"Are you okay, Kidd?" he asked. He put his hands on my upper arms and I leaned back against him.

I pointed out the window. "I know him. He came to the paper today and wanted to buy my trunk."

"Are you going to sell?"

"I already did. Carl said he picked it up after I left." My phone rang again. The number was unfamiliar, but I answered it anyway.

"I know who you are," said a male voice. "I know what you did. Where is it?"

"Who is this?" I demanded. The Lexus pulled out of the hotel parking lot and crossed the street, weaving dangerously and barely avoiding oncoming traffic.

"What's he doing?" Nick asked. The movement of

the car bothered me. It wasn't reckless driving. It was as if the driver lost control. I ran outside and waved my hands above my head to get Ronnie's attention. He drove past me and ran into a tree.

I approached the car and yanked open the door. Ronnie was slumped against the steering wheel. I pressed my fingers into the flesh of his neck. There was no pulse.

The car hadn't been going fast enough for the airbag to deploy, but that didn't seem to matter. Ronnie Holiday was dead.

5

LIMP AND LIFELESS

RONNIE'S BODY LEANED TOWARD ME AND THEN SLID out of the car. In one hand he held the Modifiers album. In the other he held his phone. The name on the phone's display, the caller ID, was mine. Not April May, because that might have made sense. The name on the screen was Samantha Kidd.

Unless Carl had told him, Ronnie Holiday had no way of knowing April May and Samantha Kidd were the same person, and even less way of knowing that person was me. The phone fell from his hand. I put my foot on top of it and eased it backward, away from his body. I dropped down to one knee, pretending to tie my sneaker, and then slipped the phone into my pocket.

Nick called the police. There wasn't much to be done for a driver who ran into a tree. There was a bump on his forehead. I didn't want to connect his death to the trunk, but it seemed impossible not to. And now the trunk was in his car. The very same trunk that could be traced back to me through auction records.

My fingers, deep inside my pocket, closed around his phone. It too connected me to Ronnie. I pulled it out and stared at the screen. The call was so recent the phone hadn't yet slipped into lock mode. Before I thought twice, I opened the YouTube app and searched for my cat's favorite video of fish. I found one that was eleven hours long that would keep the phone from going into sleep mode and requiring a passcode to unlock it. I slipped the phone back into my pocket.

As I stood in the lot, the doors to The Pho opened and Petra Moon, the owner, came out. Her gray hair cut was neatly in a pixie and wore a boxy sweater and knit pants. "Come with me," she said. She put her arm around me and guided me toward the benches out front of the restaurant. "Let the medical technicians do their jobs."

"He's dead," I said. "No one can save him."

"No, they can't. But you've seen what he's seen, haven't you? Right now, we have to think about you."

I was in a fog. Petra's words didn't make sense, but they didn't *not* make sense either. Her arm tightened around my shoulders in a protective manner. I grabbed her arm for support. Under her boxy sweater, she was solid muscle. I didn't doubt for a second that she could take care of herself. She joined me on the bench. I didn't feel much like talking, but I appreciated her company.

When the Emergency crew arrived, Nick spoke to

them briefly. He nodded and then came over to me. "Go home, Kidd," Nick said. "I'll take care of this."

"No," I protested. I pointed to Ronnie. "I know him. He came into the paper today. I should talk to someone. If anybody leaves, it should be you. You're traveling tomorrow."

"I can manage an afternoon on a plane. We'll wait together."

I offered a tentative smile to Petra. She smiled back and stood, gesturing to her seat for Nick. He took her place and reached out for my hand. I intertwined my fingers with his and watched while an ambulance crew draped a thick, black blanket over Ronnie's body.

There was a time when Nick might have cautioned me to stay out of trouble, but that changed when Nick brought trouble to our door. The experience brought our relationship to a new level. I accepted that his work was his life, and he accepted that my curious streak led me into unsavory situations. Some might say the masks were dropped and we saw each other clearly.

We stayed at The Pho until well after eleven. We'd eaten little more than the complimentary bread, but despite Petra's offer to comp our meal, my appetite was gone.

————

When we arrived home, there was a Maserati parked in the driveway. Only one person I knew owned a Maserati, though I couldn't imagine why Nick's dad was at our house at eleven o'clock at night. Nick parked next to the Maserati and I parked along the street.

"Did you know your dad was coming over?" I asked Nick as we approached the front door.

"No. He probably wanted it to be a surprise."

If the Maserati in the driveway was a surprise, the suitcases inside the front door were even more so.

Nick Senior, known simply as Senior around us because I refused to call Nick "Junior," had the body of a seventy-year old and the mind of a twenty-something. In the past year, he'd bought a sports car, adopted a French bulldog, and redecorated his apartment. He held a weekly poker game, belonged to the local vintners' club, and believed Sophia Loren was his destiny.

Senior came down the stairs. He wore a V-neck nightshirt printed with soccer balls. "Where've you been?" Senior asked. "I thought you'd be in bed by now."

"If you thought that, then why are you here?" Nick asked. "It's after eleven. It's a little late for a social call." Nick's dad was always welcome in our house, but it was a valid point.

"You're leaving tomorrow," Senior said.

Nick's face softened. "It's only for a week, dad. Samantha's going to be here to take care of anything you need."

"What do you think I am, stupid? I know she'll be here. That's why I brought Bardot."

Bardot was Senior's black French bulldog. She was curled up on the sofa next to Logan, my black cat, making it difficult to tell where one ended and the other one started. When Bardot was a puppy, I'd once caught Logan grooming him, which ranked among the most adorable things I'd ever seen in my life.

Bardot was the perfect companion for a man in his seventies. She didn't require long walks, didn't shed, made very few dog noises, and loved to go for rides. She ate a high quality diet which Nick Senior prepared for her twice a day and thrived on personal contact. Logan could turn the hallway closet into a two-day getaway, but Bardot needed companionship.

"Dad, nobody thinks you're stupid," Nick said. "But I'm still not clear on what you're doing here."

"You're going to Italy, right? To meet with Blak Friiday? You have a full schedule of factory tours and photo shoots, and dinners with Italian models, right?"

Nick's eyes cut to mine on this last point. I pretended not to smile.

With each question, Senior's intention became clear. Nick's eyes moved from Senior's face to the suitcases lined up against the wall and then back to his dad's face. I stepped backward in an attempt to leave the room and the predictable argument but Nick grabbed my arm and held me in place.

"No," Nick said, which wasn't the answer to the question about whether Nick was going to Italy, but I suspected it was the answer to what Senior was about to propose.

"I haven't been to Italy since I broke my hip. What that been, five years? I booked a last-minute saver fare. Called up the airline and charmed my way into a first-class ticket." Senior winked at me and then grinned at Nick. "Your old man's still got it."

Nick turned to me. "Help."

I stepped forward. "You don't want to schlep to Italy for a shoe show, do you?"

"You're right. I don't want to go to Italy for a shoe show. I want to hang out with Blak Friiday, drink Barolo, and eat my weight in ossobuco."

"You can do all of that here if you time it right."

"Have you ever ordered ossobuco in Ribbon?" he asked. He took my lack of response as a response. "Exactly. Kiddo, I'm not getting any younger. My doctor has me watching my cholesterol, and I just had a screening last week. My days of wine and veal are numbered."

I had to give him credit. He'd thought this through.

Senior grabbed the smallest of his suitcases and pulled it to the stairs. "Guest bedroom okay?" he asked, ignoring Nick's protests.

Nick nodded, though I wasn't sure he'd even heard the question. He appeared to have been on the receiving end of a stun gun. "My dad's coming to Italy," he said after Senior was out of earshot. "Isn't that great?"

"It's great," I repeated. Positive mantras and all.

Nick kissed me, and the kiss went from gentle peck to an invitation to go upstairs, providing the perfect end to a not-perfect day.

Sunlight woke me shortly after six. Nick was wide awake and staring at the ceiling. "I have to cancel this trip," Nick said. No "good morning," no "hey, sleepyhead," no "roll over and go back to sleep." I got the feeling he'd been staring at the ceiling all night willing me to wake up.

The world of celebrity can be an inconvenient place. After signing the contract, it looked as though scheduling conflicts were going to push their collaboration into next year. Then Blak mentioned in passing that he had a four-day gap on his Italian tour. Nick booked a ticket and a film crew immediately. Basically, he was traveling four thousand miles to shoot an ad campaign with a person who lived sixty miles away.

"You can't cancel. Who knows when Blak's schedule will open back up? Besides, you're booked with factory appointments and leather houses."

"But my dad's a full-time job. You know what he's like."

"Have him take Bardot."

Nick shifted onto his side and propped his head on his hand. "Bardot's going to require—"

"—regular trips outside of the venue for walks, potty breaks, and food."

He looked at me. It was a clever idea and he knew it; his dad would never suspect Bardot was a foil.

"We have to leave earlier than I planned so I can get her carrier and medication." Nick picked up his phone from the nightstand and checked the time. Normally when Nick headed out of town he booked an afternoon flight so we could have a proper goodbye, but there were multiple reasons why that wasn't going to happen today. "His apartment is the opposite direction of the airport."

"I'll run to his place and get Bardot's things."

"Thanks, Kidd. You're a doll." He reinforced his thanks with a kiss that made us both forget what he'd just said about time.

———

An hour later, I dressed in a high-necked white T-shirt and short black skort with black ankle booties that originally belonged to my mother in the sixties. My recent closet purge did not extend to items of a historic nature, mostly because I was always prepared for the question, "Do you still have my Bernardos?" Under the booties, I wore little white socklets that weren't visible, but kept my pinky toe from rubbing up against the inside of the suede. I grabbed my keys and left. My car was still parked along the street. The trunk was wide open. Had I accidentally hit the trunk release?

It wasn't until I closed the trunk that I noticed scratches in the paint. My open trunk wasn't due to negligence. Someone had picked the lock.

6

WE HAVE A PROBLEM

I WASN'T IN THE HABIT OF DRIVING AROUND WITH valuables in the trunk of my car, so with the exception of a receipt from the wine store and a windshield scraper, the trunk was empty. Anyone who knew me knew that, and anyone who didn't would have been disappointed. Still, I couldn't shake the feeling that this wasn't a random act of vandalism.

Twenty minutes later, I pulled into the parking lot to Senior's apartment and parked in a visitor space. I'd spent enough time there to be comfortable with the layout, but it never ceased to delight how a seventy-something bachelor lived. Nick's mom died when Nick was still young, so it had been two of them for a long time. The apartment, originally Nick's, now housed his dad, and with that came subtle changes like the "Ladies of Italy" wall calendar tacked above his desk. There were other signs of his interest: financial magazines on the coffee table, a fridge filled with Peroni, a leather recliner aimed at the large-screen TV, and a DVD library filled with buddy cop movies. Don't judge a book by its cover, I say.

Notes from the property manager were wedged between the doorknob and door frame of each unit in the hallway. I took the one from Senior's place and carried it inside, then unfolded it and read. It was a notice that they would be conducting inspections of the smoke detectors over the next two days. I set the paper on the counter and collected Bardot's leash, medication, and favorite blanket. I called Nick when I was ready to leave.

"I'm done here. There's a note about smoke detectors on the front door. Is your dad okay with them entering while he's gone?"

"Dad?" Nick called out. His voice muffled for a moment and then he said, "you what?" Some heated back-and-forth took place and then Nick returned to the call.

"We have a problem. I'll spare you the exact quote. It seems my dad took the batteries out of his smoke detectors for his last poker game. Dad, hold on."

The phone changed hands and Senior's voice replaced Nick's. "Kiddo, my new property owner is a nosy nelly. If she thinks I'm out of town during this inspection, she's going to go through my things. Junior, what are you doing?"

"Dad, go to your room," Nick said. A moment later, he said, "are you there?"

"Did that work?"

"If you think of the second floor landing as his room, then it did. He's been warned about the smoke detectors multiple times. If they catch him again, he's in violation of his lease. You know what that means."

This wasn't the first time the idea of Senior moving in came up. We had the space, especially now that I no longer used the spare bedroom as a walk-in closet, and if we started a family like we sometimes discussed, it would be handy to have his help. But as Nick's business took off, all of the above conversations stalled.

"I'm on it." I glanced at the paper on the counter. "Inspections are today and tomorrow. They're starting with the next building over so I can't predict when they'll get here."

Nick asked. "Hold on."

"Me or him?" I asked.

"You. What?"

"I didn't say anything," I said.

"Not you. What?"

This ranked among my least productive conversations. I wandered to the window and stared down at the parking lot ten stories below. Most of the residents paid an additional fee for covered parking, so the lot was only partially full. My limited edition Refraction Blue Toyota Supra stood out amongst more generic silver and white cars. Buying it was the result of a spontaneous decision at the end of a massive amount of deliberation, and aside from the inability to go undercover, I was happy with my choice.

"Are you still there?" Nick asked.

"Me this time?" I asked.

"Yes, you."

"Yes, I'm here."

"Are you working at the paper today?"

"I was going to. Why?"

"Can you work from his place instead?"

I was still a little burned up by Carl's practical joke and wouldn't mind the excuse to work remotely. I glanced up at the clock. "I need to get a few things from the office, but I can work from here."

"Thanks, Kidd. We'll swing by for Bardot's things shortly."

I hadn't thought much about work since Nick's dad showed up at our house last night. Twelve hours ago, I been expecting to write about the trunk, but now that I'd sold it to Ronnie, I was without an assignment. And with Ronnie dead, the trunk was—actually, I didn't know where the trunk was. Had Ronnie had it in the car with him when he drove into the tree? Or had he delivered it to the man in the leather jacket who'd tried to take it from the *Ribbon Eagle* offices? He had driven through the Kirkville Hotel parking lot before crossing the street. I had more questions about the trunk now than I did when I first bought it.

I slipped my hand into the pocket of my skort and pulled out Ronnie's phone. The battery was low from running the fish video for the past eight hours, so I plugged it in and swiped the button back to the beginning to restart the video. I then considered wiping my name from the recent call logs and pitching the phone in the trash. Probably not a great idea. If Ronnie's death was anything more than a car accident, his phone might include a lead other than me. But as long as I had access...

I cued up the recent call logs. Mine was the most recent number called, but in the past week, Ronnie had been busy. There were twelve calls in the past twenty four hours.

Three recent calls were from the *Ribbon Eagle*. One was from me. I knew because I'd told him I would sell but someone at the paper had been in contact with him long before he showed up asking for me.

I didn't recognize the other numbers. I made a list of the call log and tucked it into the pocket of my trench coat, left a love note for Nick with Bardot's things, then grabbed my keys and left.

It was my untested theory that you could get from one end of Ribbon to the other in twenty minutes. The newspaper office was on the west side near Senior's apartment. Door to door it was eleven and a half.

Most of my coworkers arrived around nine. Monty wasn't a stickler for punching a clock; he cared more about productivity and output. Carl spent ninety percent of his time in the field but turned out story after story by deadline. The obituaries required him to stop in daily since they came in through a secure server to which Monty refused remote access.

It was eight thirty-seven when I entered the building. José was in the lobby. "Morning, Samantha," he said. "Two days in a row! That's a record. I thought you'd be at home plotting revenge on Carl after yesterday's stunt."

"You heard about that?"

He smiled sheepishly. "I may have been in on it."

I put my hands over my heart and stumbled backward as if he'd shot me. "José. You're on Carl's team? Say it ain't so."

"I'm an equal opportunity gun for hire." He grinned, flashing crooked teeth framed out in an engaging smile. "Any plans to get him back?"

I thought for a moment. "You know how Carl loves his desk?"

"Yes."

"Could you swap out the legs and then sand them down by a quarter of an inch every day after he leaves?"

José smiled. "You're diabolical." He smiled. "Consider it done."

QUITE THE INVESTIGATIVE
REPORTER

I left José and went to the second floor. The bullpen was quiet. Any traces of the anniversary party had been placed in waste baskets and lined up in the hallway. I walked past a row of putty-colored bins and went inside. I was the first one there.

There wasn't time to waste. I went to my cubicle and packed up my laptop, then opened my desk drawer and put the cigar box on my desk. It was the only thing I had left from the trunk.

Before I could think further about it, the elevator door pinged and Carl came in. I jammed the cigar box into my computer bag before he could see them.

Carl wore his trademark seersucker suit and white leather sneakers, with a brown leather messenger bag slung over his shoulder. He narrowed his eyes and looked at my desk. "I didn't expect you to show your face after yesterday's embarrassment." He raised his hands to his face and pantomimed fear.

"José already told me he was in on it," I said. "Just remember, turnabout is fair play."

"Bring it on, Kidd." He walked to the back row of computers and dumped his bag on his chair, then opened his bag and pulled out a thick envelope. "Here," he said, extending it to me.

"What's that?"

"You didn't think I was going to leave fifty grand in your desk, did you?"

I glanced at the envelope. "I thought you gave it to Monty."

"Why would I give it to him? It's yours."

"It's for the paper. To keep us afloat until we can get subscriber numbers back up."

"Are you kidding me?" Carl tossed the envelope at me and I caught it. "The paper's doing better than ever. Oswald's got a knack for advertising sales. Why do you think Monty wants more articles? He needs more pages so he can sell more ad space. Subscriptions are at an all-time high ever since that series on denim got syndicated."

Carl was referring to a four-part series I wrote after attempting to join a secret fashion society as their denim expert. As far as I knew, the society disbanded, but it could be they reformed and my invitation got lost in the mail.

"If we're doing so well, then why is this place filled with unpaid interns?"

"Because there's a college across the street." He pointed to the window. "You're quite the investigative reporter. Who's your source? The girls who sell cookies in the lobby?"

I wedged the envelope of cash into my handbag and zipped it shut. Even though my source was arguably the most reliable person at the paper, if we were in trouble, Carl would know.

"Tell Monty I'm working from home today," I said. I turned around and left.

"No can do. Staff meeting at three. Don't even think about skipping it. You need to pitch a new story." He unscrewed the lid of his Thermos and dumped steaming coffee into a chipped mug. "See you later, Kidd."

I grabbed everything I thought I'd need to work from Senior's and left with Carl's laughter ringing in my ears. I didn't know why Monty would lie about the paper's financial position, but now I had two mysteries to solve. I also had to get back to Senior's and reconnect the smoke detectors. When it rains, it pours, and I felt a storm coming.

I stopped at the drug store for a value-pack of batteries and then grabbed a bagel sandwich at Dough Re Mi, the bakery next door. When I returned to Senior's place, the puppy stuff was gone. Nick had added a response to my love note: *Sorry I missed you. Will be back before you know it. XO* I ran my index finger over the X's and O's, then folded the note in half and slipped it into my handbag.

Maybe it was because Nick and I first met through work: him as a designer of ladies' shoes and me as his buyer, and we established our relationship through client dinners and market appointments in the various cities where the designer shoe business took place, but once we came together, his travel schedule hadn't been an issue. He kept an apartment in Milan that he sublet periodically, and more recently added in trips to China to research production his new sneaker line. I used to wonder how things would change after we started a family, but we'd recently learned that Nick suffered from low motility, and I had a hostile uterus. For everything that made us feel like we were made for each other, this one incompatibility told me the universe had a sense of humor.

I fortified myself with two bites of the bagel sandwich, tackled the smoke detectors, and then set up a makeshift workstation at the dining room table. I didn't want to pitch another story. From the moment I learned about the Boyd Brighton Mod Auction, I'd been thinking about the contents of that trunk and what it might tell me about the owner.

Mod was my favorite era of fashion. The graphic black and white, the clean lines, heavy inspiration from the art scene at the time, all pleased me in a way that bohemian and the later hippie movement did not. It was a time when men indulged in suits that they tailored to fit them closely and then covered their designer suits in parkas to keep them from getting dirty. Few trends could be traced back to the geopolitical landscape at the time like mod; the trend connected strongly with the emerging youth culture that shed their reliance on parents with jobs to fund clothing to assert their identity and scooter purchases to declare their independence. And while other trends have come and gone, the mod movement became more than a way to dress. It was a state of mind and it never went away.

I pulled the cigar box out of my handbag and opened it. Inside was a pair of Ray-Ban Wayfarer sunglasses on top of a dog-eared copy of *I'm OK – You're OK,* the late sixties self-help book. I turned the book over in my hands and then set it aside. Under the book was a paisley cravat, one loose cuff, and an assortment of passports.

I picked up one of the passports and flipped it open. The picture was of Boyd Brighton, but the name was not. It was issued in the UK. I opened another passport and saw the same photo, but again, the name was different. A low-level buzzy sensation filled my body while I opened the third, fourth, and fifth. Each passport indicated a different country of issue. A different name. And the same photograph.

I set the passports down and picked up the cufflink, slowly turning it over in my hand. The design was a tarnished gold disc with a jet stone in the middle. The stone appeared to be loose. I ran my finger over it and then pressed and a tiny metal dart flew out and embedded into the arm of Senior's recliner.

A cold sensation ran through my limbs. This cigar box had been inside a trunk I'd purchased for fifty dollars, but I no longer felt the attempted theft of it or the death of the man I'd sold it to were accidental. I crossed the room, pulled the dart out from the fabric of the recliner, and ran my finger over the sharp, pointy tip.

If I were looking at what I thought I was looking at, then the owner of the trunk might not just have been a part of the music industry.

He might have been a spy.

8

OPERATION SMOKE DETECTOR

THE FIRST RULE OF JOURNALISM WAS, WELL, THE FIRST rule of journalism was to truth and accuracy, but somewhere on the list—number four, maybe? —was humanity. I didn't need to have the trunk in my possession to write a human interest story about a once-famous musician, but this new discovery led to questions about Boyd. Everything I'd heard about him was that he'd been the lead singer of a middling mod band over fifty years ago and that he walked away from it at the peak of his celebrity. But this—well, this told me something completely different.

It wasn't every day I got to liken fashion with intellectual pursuits. I had a degree in fashion history, and the relationship between historical events and the clothes people wore was incontrovertible. Often, it was the look of an era that caught my attention, but the thrill came in understanding why those looks mattered. There was always a story behind the style.

I tried to ignore it. And for four minutes, I succeeded. I opened a file on my computer to brainstorm replacement articles for "Untying the Mysteries of Ribbon." But I couldn't concentrate. To the rest of the world, Ronnie died in a car crash. But now, I wasn't so sure.

I opened a new document and typed:

NOTES ABOUT MYSTERY TRUNK:

1. BOYD BRIGHTON AUCTION
2. VALUABLE TO PEOPLE WHO DIDN'T WANT TO BUY AT AUCTION
3. CONTAINS POSSIBLE 50+YEAR OLD EVIDENCE OF ESPIONAGE

NEXT, I WROTE:

FACTS ABOUT RONNIE HOLIDAY:

1. OWNER OF NEW MOD SHOP
2. OVERPAID FOR MYSTERY TRUNK
3. DROVE INTO A TREE

IT WASN'T A LOT TO GO ON.

I checked the clock. It was close to ten. Inspections at the apartment building were underway, and Operation Smoke Detector was not one I could abort if I wanted to maintain marital harmony. I needed to clone myself, but since cloning technology hadn't made its way to Ribbon, I did the next best thing. I called Eddie.

"Dude," he answered.

"Are you busy?"

"I just left Borough Hall. The building is graffiti-free. Do you want to grab lunch?"

"I can't. I'm in the middle of some covert activity, and I need your help."

Eddie's voice dropped to a whisper. "Do you think it's safe to discuss covert activity on the phone?"

"Good point. Meet me at Nick Senior's apartment and I'll fill you in when you get here."

Professionally, Eddie was in the top one percent of his field. He often grumbled at the creative process, but I'd watched him produce outstanding merchandising displays, an over-the-top exhibit at the local museum, and a British-themed birthday party for a newly-divorced, about-to-retire, curmudgeonly homicide detective who now ran a private investigation firm. (I use the term "firm" loosely since his office sits between a Chinese takeout restaurant and a dentist.)

Eddie showed up within the hour. I identified him through the peephole, but when I opened the door, I pinched his cheek for good measure. He swatted my hand away.

"What was that for?"

I led him inside. "I'm living a *Mission Impossible* plot. I had to make sure you weren't somebody wearing a rubber Eddie mask."

"This is why we're friends." He flopped onto Senior's recliner and put up his feet. "You're certifiable, and I do nothing to encourage you to seek professional help. It's the perfect codependent alliance."

Eddie had a collection of message tees, and today he wore one that said PHILLY VS. EVERYBODY. I made a fresh pot of coffee and caught Eddie up on the last twenty-for hours, starting with the delivery of the trunk.

"Only you would get excited about junk in a trunk."

"You just said we had the basis for the perfect codependent friendship, right?"

"I said—"

I held up my hand. "I know what you said. You know what you said. And you're right. That's why you're here. There's more going on than meets the eye, at least I think, but if I tell anyone else, they're going to have me locked up."

Eddie leaned back and crossed his arms over his chest. He tipped his head to the side and assessed me. This was familiar territory and I knew how it usually played out: him weighing whether or not he had the time or inclination to indulge in my theories, real or imagined.

"If you're that worried about incriminating yourself, do you think it's safe to talk here? The place might be bugged."

I scanned the apartment. There was absolutely no reason to suspect someone was listening in, but it seemed wise to be prudent. I pulled my notepad closer to me and wrote "Bug killer" on my shopping list. "Follow me into the bathroom," I said.

Eddie didn't move. "We don't have that kind of relationship."

I rolled my eyes and carried the cigar box to the bathroom. I turned on the sink and the shower faucets and leaned back against the towel rack. Eddie peeked inside. He shook his head and entered.

"You're never boring, I'll give you that."

I dropped onto the only seat in the room. Fortunately, the lid was down. "Technically, I never opened the trunk. The janitor from the building cut off the padlock, but before I looked inside, Ronnie Holiday showed up asking for me. I mean, he asked for April May."

"That's you, right? Is that significant?"

"I don't know. My editor told me to meet with Ronnie, and when he left, the trunk was unlocked and one of the interns had unpacked some items to photograph."

"So you *did* go into it."

"I didn't."

"You can't trick me with technicalities like you do the rest of the world."

"You know, when I talk to Nick about stuff like this, he's a lot more understanding."

Eddie looked over one shoulder, then he looked over the other. He stood up and poked his head into the shower, and then dropped the curtain and turned back. "I don't see Nick here, do you?"

"Nick and his dad are in Italy, or they will be soon. They've got a full schedule with Bardot and Blak Friiday, and I don't need to pile my suspicions on top of that dance card."

"It's nice how you and Nick trust each other."

"It is, right?" I thought for a moment. "Remind me to hide evidence of my recent binge-eating before he comes home."

Eddie snorted.

"Long story short: Nobody knows I took this cigar box from the trunk If nobody knew what was in it, then they'd never know it wasn't there, right?"

"I suppose that's sound logic," Eddie said. "What was in it?"

"These," I said. I flipped the box open and handed Eddie the passports. He opened and shut three of them and then handed them back. "So?"

I picked up the cufflink and pressed the black stone. A dart flew past Eddie and embedded in the wall.

I lowered my voice. "I think Boyd Brighton was a spy."

He lowered his voice too. "Dude, it's been sixty years. I think your intel might be outdated."

That was the thing. Even if I had found evidence that Boyd was a spy, who would care? The only person it might affect was him, and he was already dead. The information would mean little more than an update to his Wikipedia page.

"Should I call the C.I.A.? Do you think something from this trunk is a threat to national security?"

Eddie picked up a paisley cravat from the pile of men's clothes. "Maybe you should call U.N.C.L.E."

I snatched the cravat from his hands and ran my thumb back and forth over the intricate paisley pattern. The texture was coarse, silk shot through with horsehair to give it structure. It seemed odd to have found a stash of men's clothes hidden in the bottom of the trunk of an unknown female, but that was the least curious part of the trunk's mystery.

I leaned against the back of the toilet. "Last night, after you left the restaurant, the owner of the mod shop drove into a tree. It was like he just lost consciousness while driving and ran into the corner in the parking lot. The airbag didn't even deploy. If the coroner determines the cause of death was natural, then that's it. No reason for a homicide investigation or an autopsy."

"Can't you call Patti?"

Eddie was referring to Patti Detweiler, the Berks County Coroner. I'd met her last year while embroiled in a murder related to a secret fashion society. She was the first female coroner in the history of the city, a statistic that made people think twice about approaching her in public. People don't mess with lady coroners.

"I could," I said, "but I don't want to raise any red flags. If Ronnie's death isn't considered suspicious, then she'll sign off on the death certificate and call it a day."

"I don't want to be a spoilsport here, but your name in a dead person's recently called list is going to raise a red flag. This won't fly under the radar."

I stood up and reached into the pocket of my skort and pulled out Ronnie's phone. I held it up, wiggled it back and forth, and then set it on the lid of the toilet where I'd just been.

"Did you get a new phone?" Eddie asked.

"No."

"I didn't think so."

The good thing about discussing choices of this nature with Eddie was that I didn't have to spell out the details. He knew me well enough to know the sort of decisions I made—the same sort most people might think were not in my best interest, but those people aren't here so let's leave them out of it, okay? —and not waste time with a lecture.

After an awkward silence (where Eddie *may* have been considering a lecture thereby forever altering the course of our friendship), I said, "The way I see it, there's no connection between me and Ronnie anymore. I put a padlock on the trunk and he took it. Nobody knows I took anything out."

The doorbell rang and I looked at Eddie with wide eyes. "Somebody's here," I mouthed.

"Answer it," Eddie mouthed back.

I turned the water and the shower off and we returned to the living room. The steam had left my skin dewy. I tiptoed to the door and peered out the peephole. Petra stood on the other side. I opened the door.

"Hi Sam," She looked past me. "Is Senior around?"

"He went to Italy with Nick. Last minute trip."

"So he's feeling better?" she asked.

"I didn't know he was ill."

"Probably allergies," she said dismissively. "It couldn't be serious if he was able to travel." She tried to look past me. "Are you puppy sitting?" She made kissy noises.

"Bardot's not here. He took her with him. Senior wanted me here when the property manager comes through."

Petra chucked. "Those smoke detectors are going to get him evicted."

"Not on my watch." I grinned.

She held a tinfoil covered block in her hands. "Your father-in-law is one of my taste testers." She held the tinfoil block out. "This is Vietnamese honeycomb cake. It's green, so I'm hoping it will appeal to our Irish customers as well."

I took the bundle. It was still warm. I held it up to my nose and sniffed. It smelled faintly sweet with a tinge of coconut. "I can't wait to try it."

"Let me know what you think." She glanced down the hall. "I just stopped by to tell him—to tell *you*, I guess—the property manager is running behind. She started with the other building. She won't get to us until tomorrow."

"Thanks for the heads up."

I closed the door behind her. Before I had a chance to set the honeycomb cake on the kitchen counter, there was another knock on the door. I opened the door without looking through the peephole. Petra was still there.

"Me again," she said. She seemed nervous. "Can I come in for a second?"

"Sure," I backed away from the door, and she entered. "Is everything okay?"

She pointed to the tinfoil block tucked under my arm. "Your father-in-law isn't a taste tester. I made that so I'd have an excuse to come down here and talk to you."

"But you didn't know I was here."

She pointed to the window. "I saw you from the parking lot."

I walked to the kitchen and set the honeycomb cake on the counter. "What's going on, Petra?"

The normally perky restaurant owner appeared nervous. "Did the police talk to you? About the man who drove into the tree?"

"The police don't investigate car accidents, especially when a person drives into a tree."

She bit her lip and scanned the room, looking everywhere but at me. I could see why she didn't join the weekly poker game. She finally made eye contact. "I know about you. Nick Senior told Phil about you at a poker game. When Ronnie drove into that tree, I knew you were going to ask questions. I was scared you'd find out...I knew him."

"Ronnie owned the store next to your restaurant, so I assumed you knew him."

"I didn't just know him. He ate in the restaurant."

"Makes sense," I said. I still couldn't see why Petra was so concerned.

"I just—wanted you to know. So it doesn't seem like I'm hiding anything."

"Petra, what exactly did Nick's dad tell Phil?"

"That you make it a point to find out people's secrets."

"What was the context?"

"Phil said you seemed nice."

Leave it to Nick's dad to hear a perfectly good compliment and twist it into something else! I put my arm around Petra. "I have a feeling my father-in-law was trying to intimidate Phil into showing his hand." I smiled genuinely. "Accidents happen. I saw the whole thing. The restaurant wasn't at fault."

Petra nodded her head. "I just wanted you to know," she said again. She pointed to the cake. "Hope you enjoy the cake." She left again, and this time didn't come back.

The pantry in the kitchen opened, and Eddie stepped out. He dusted some flour from the shoulder of his Philly T-shirt. He caught me staring and shrugged. "Dude, if you're right about everything you told me this morning, then it's better nobody knows I was here."

"It was Petra," I said. "I don't think she would have minded."

"Right. But she'd probably wonder why I was hiding in the pantry."

"Nobody told you to—never mind."

I unpeeled the Vietnamese honeycomb cake and cut two slices. The interior of the bread was a cheerful shade of green with air pockets to keep it light. The scent of coconut ballooned through the kitchen. For the next five minutes, the only sounds in the apartment were related to eating something tasty.

When we finished eating and cleaning the counter, I went to the sofa and sat down. Eddie tapped the damaged copy of *I'm OK - You're OK*. "I thought you were off self-help."

Eddie was referring to my on-again/off-again relationship with personal growth. In my quest to discover what I wanted out of life, I've employed a life coach, called a personal growth podcast, Marie Kondo'd my closets, and turned over more new leaves than an autumn gale storm. Ultimately, I'd decided to take a more passive approach to life and go with the flow, which now that I thought about it wasn't working out all that well.

"It's not mine," I said. A business card that had been stuck to the back fell off. ~~London~~, ~~Paris~~, ~~Milan~~, Ribbon. I flipped it over. It was the card Ronnie left with me when he stopped by the paper.

Eddie glanced at the card. "Did The Mod Holiday open yet? It's that revolving storefront next to The Pho."

I sat up. "That's right. You were thinking about working there, right? What did you tell them?"

"That I can't start until I finish this job for the city. At that location, they'll probably be out of business before Christmas."

Eddie didn't know it, but he'd just given me an idea.

Since I no longer had a trunk of clothes to write about, I needed an idea to pitch at the staff meeting. Covering a new mod boutique, especially one owned by the dead man who bought my mystery trunk seemed as good an idea as any.

9

JUNE JULY

THE MOD HOLIDAY WAS A FREESTANDING STORE ON Perkiomen Avenue. They shared a parking lot with The Pho. Between growing up in Ribbon and then moving back, I'd watched half a dozen businesses move into and out of this location, and I had no reason to believe this one would last. But Ronnie Holiday had been their creative director, and I wanted to know more about him. Monty would have supported the suggestion if I'd asked him, I was almost completely sure of it.

The lot was empty except for a dirty white sedan parked at the far end next to a long, orange roll-off dumpster. It was overflowing with broken down brown cardboard boxes and black plastic garbage bags stretched to capacity. A breeze idled through my window and tossed my hair around my face while the sun beat down on my left arm. The air had a faint edge of exhaust fumes from passing motorists.

I turned my ringer to silent and went into the shop.

The interior was bright white, the occasional colorful vintage poster advertising bands and movies from the sixties. Silver rounders—the circular fixtures that stores often use to display clearance items—sat around the interior, with clear plexiglass sign holders atop indicating sizes. One rack was marked "Birds" and another with "Blokes."

Having spent a considerable amount of time working in retail, I tuned into more than just the contents of the store. The bones of a great shopping experience were there, but overall, it looked more like a temporary fire sale than a shop with a clear point of view. I flipped over the price tag of a shift dress from the Birds rack, surprised to see it was six hundred dollars. They were never going to move merchandise at this price if they displayed it like the clearance racks at Marshalls.

A door behind the register area opened and a woman walked through. She was petite, dressed in a black and white checkered, A-line dress with white tights and white boots. She wore her thick hair in a bob that was flipped under, though instead of hanging neatly, static electricity caused one side to defy gravity. Her tights had a smudge of discoloration across the knee that matched a second smudge on the hem of her dress. She held a box that seemed to test the limits of what she was able to carry by herself, and she leaned backward to counter the weight. When she saw me, she dropped the box, and several small plastic packages of colorful tights fell out onto the floor.

"Hi," she said. "Welcome to The Mod Holiday. I'm

Franny." For a moment, she seemed conflicted between leaving me unattended in the shop and walking back out the door from which she'd come. "I'm juggling deliverymen by the loading area." She pointed over her shoulder. "I'm alone today so I have to handle them, but I'll be back in a moment. If you have any questions, give me a holler."

"Sure," I said. Franny went back through the door and left me alone to snoop.

I made my way toward the front of the shop. A mess of cardboard boxes covered the floor behind the counter, similar to the one she just carried in, all opened and exposing colorful items of dress. A steamer in the corner released a thin trickle of hot, damp air into the store. I knew enough about retail to know Franny's day was going to be full whether she had any customers or not. I also knew nothing she did inside the store would make a darn bit of difference if she didn't find customers to walk through that door. Something inside me lit up, a glimmer of confidence about this world I'd once inhabited, and it surprised me to realize that I missed it. After all this time. Who knew? And when Franny reappeared through the doorway, I stepped forward and initiated the plan I'd conceived in the parking lot.

"Are you looking for anything special?" she asked.

"I'm here to see the creative director about a job. Is Ronnie Holiday available?"

"What job?" she asked.

"Visual merchandising."

"Uncle Ronnie's gone," Franny said.

My body tense up at her cavalier attitude. "He left?" I asked mostly to keep her talking. "We talked about this job a few days ago. He told me to come in today."

"Uncle Ronnie's never been the most reliable person, but this wasn't the sort of trip a person plans for," Franny said. "But if he hired you, then he finally did something right before he died."

If her cavalier attitude had left me unsure about whether she knew, this last statement cleared up my confusion. "I'm so sorry for your loss," I said.

"Don't be. Aside from money on a balance sheet, we weren't close." She leaned down on her elbows. "What's your name?"

I froze. What name should I give: Samantha Kidd? April May? Agent 99?

"June July," I said.

"Welcome to the team, June. When can you start?"

I had nothing on my agenda until my afternoon staff meeting at the paper. Nick was out of town, Eddie was working on citywide beautification, and Logan had fresh bowls of cat food and water. I was a woman with nothing but free time. "Um, right now?"

"Great. Can you watch the store while I get the last of the deliveries?"

"Sure." I flipped through a tray of earrings while Franny went back through the door, and then used the steamer to smooth out the creases on a rack of recently unpacked dresses. I was so absorbed in my task that I didn't hear Franny return, and I jumped when she dropped something on the floor behind me.

"Sorry if I startled you," Franny said. "That was heavier than I expected."

I turned around, but it wasn't Franny that caught my attention. It was a trunk.

The trunk.

"What's that?" I asked. Samantha Kidd and April May might have recognized it, but June July was an innocent new employee with an inquisitive side.

"Uncle Ronnie must have bought it at the Boyd Brighton auction. I told him not to bother. It's probably junk. Honestly, there's so much to do to get the store up and running that whatever's in there is the least of my concerns."

I pushed the trunk to the back wall and set a stack of scooter helmets on top. It seemed too big of a coincidence for the trunk to arrive at Ronnie's store where I now worked (let's not be sticklers for details, okay?), especially since no one at the auction house should have known that Ronnie bought the trunk off me the morning he died.

I turned back to Franny. "Who delivered it?"

"An independent delivery service."

"Aren't you curious about the contents?"

"It has a padlock on it," she said, as if that were a deterrent. "Besides, there's a lot of work to do, especially now." She dismissed the trunk as if it were a minor disruption to her day and nothing more.

One by one I steamed dresses while Franny sat on a stool behind the register and pulled a plastic package out of the box in front of her. She tore the plastic open and set a neatly folded red and white striped T-shirt on the counter and reached for another. Franny's attitude didn't strike me as that of a person who'd learned that her uncle had died, but I didn't know her well enough to know what his death meant to her.

After forty-five minutes of uncomfortable silence, I asked, "Do you want to talk about him? Your uncle."

She looked up. "Uncle Ronnie's had one foot in the grave since the time I was born," she said. "Honestly? I'm not surprised he's dead. I'm surprised it took this long for his past to catch up with him."

10

AUGUST JULY

HER CHOICE OF WORDS STRUCK ME AS ODD, AND NOT from their heartlessness. To the rest of the world, Ronnie's death was an accident.

"He seemed like a nice man when he interviewed me," I said. It wasn't exactly the truth, but this didn't seem the time to stop lying.

"You must have met him on an off day," she said. "Uncle Ronnie was a bully. He wasn't even technically my uncle, but I don't think I'm supposed to know that. My mom let it slip after she had too many glasses of wine. They met at a rehab clinic when she was a teenager. He was a patient and she was a volunteer. He had no place to go, so she asked my grandparents if he could move in until he turned eighteen."

"You must have known him your whole life."

"When he was around. He hooked up with a biker gang when I was five."

"Like the guys who hang out at the Kirkville bar across the street?" I asked.

"Yes," she said with a huge sigh. "He'd come over with raw knuckles like he'd been in a fight. He'd disappear for months on end and then show up asking for money. My parents used to talk about what a burden he was on our family—not in front of me, but I would hear them through closed doors. My dad wanted him out of our lives, but my mom wouldn't turn her back on him. She said somewhere in there was a scared little boy who never got the attention he needed from his biological family."

"Your mother sounds like a compassionate woman."

"She rescues stray kittens, too." She shifted the rack in front of her and then straightened out the garments that hung on it. "After the biker gang, he turned back to drugs. When I was in high school, he showed up all strung out. They tried to make him go to rehab, but he said no."

My brain spun with this new wealth of information. Ronnie lived a storied life in and out of danger, and even his in-laws had wanted him gone. Was it possible his murder had a closer-to-home motive than the trunk?

"How does your dad feel about Ronnie's death?"

"My dad died five years ago. He was sick for a long time. I can't say it was a surprise, but it doesn't make me miss him any less." At this, her eyes welled up, and a tear spilled out. She swiped it away.

"And your mom?"

"She loved Ronnie, but she knew he was trouble. They had a falling out around the time my dad died, and as far as I know, she hasn't talked to him since."

"Where's she now?"

"On a cruise. I called her this morning, but there's not much she can do from the ocean."

"How long has she been gone?" I asked hopefully. Franny looked at me oddly. "Those cruises sound great, but I imagine a person could get tired of sleeping on a boat."

"Not my mom. It's a twenty-one day cruise around the Panama Canal. She departed from Miami two weeks ago and her friends rented a house there so they don't have to hurry home."

My hopes for an easy answer fell. In terms of alibis, it was more solid than most.

"What will happen to the store now?"

Franny held my stare. "My uncle and I had an agreement. Walls out were his responsibility and everything inside was mine. His filing system was a mess but I finally found the lease. We were going to split the profits fifty-fifty. I sank everything I have into stocking this place. I just hope business is strong enough to cover his end of the expenses."

We kept working on the new deliveries. There was enough work to make me seem busy, but before long, Franny would expect me to actually merchandise something. I needed to call for backup, and backup meant Eddie.

"Do you mind if I make a phone call?" I asked.

She waved at the phone. "Sure," she said.

I left the steamer, slipped my phone into my pocket, and went into the hallway for privacy.

"Dude," he answered.

"Hey," I said brightly. "I got the job, and I started today. Do you think you could bring me something to eat?"

"What job? I thought we were splitting a pizza when you got done working on paper stuff."

"Sure, pizza works. Bring it to The Mod Holiday. Thanks. I'll see you soon." I disconnected and immediately followed up with a text that said *I'll explain everything later.* Eddie responded with *this better be good,* and I volleyed back: *you have no idea.*

I returned to the store. Franny had unpacked all the striped T-shirts and was sorting them by size. "Everything okay?" she asked.

"Yes. I didn't expect to start today, so I had to change my plans for the night." At her expression, I held up my hand. "It's no problem. Honestly. I'm thrilled to be here." And you'll be relieved to know I *was* being honest, because if I hadn't stuck around, I might never have known about the trunk delivery!

Eddie's arrival at the store was announced by the scent of pizza. I was behind the counter, on my knees, merchandising the case lines that faced the store with bright and colorful Bakelite earrings shaped like flowers. Franny greeted Eddie with "Welcome to The Mod Holiday," then, "You must be June's friend."

"June?" Eddie asked.

"August!" I cried out. I stood up quickly and the blood rushed to my head. Eddie turned to me and the pizza box tipped to a dangerous angle. It was a good thing the cheese had had time to congeal, otherwise we'd be looking a mess when we opened the box.

"Dude," Eddie said. ("Dude" worked as a greeting, a question, a period, and in this case, a safe word.)

"Franny, this is my brother."

"Hi, August," she said. She looked back and forth between us. "You two look nothing alike."

"Different fathers," I said.

Eddie still wore his PHILLY VS. EVERYBODY T-shirt. Bright neon splatters of paint accentuated the fabric on his black cargo pants. A paint brush rested in the loop on the side of his pants where cargo pant designers anticipated a hammer going. The same neon paint colors on his pants were visible on his black and white checkered Vans, indicting the drips were less by design and more the side effect of creative work, which was dangerously close to the sort of thing that, if Franny inquired, would give away Eddie's real identity.

"Do you need a job too?" Franny asked hopefully. I was marginally insulted, as it indicated she was less than enthused with my first hour of work.

"August has a job," I said. "He's a—" I searched my mind— "pizza deliveryman," I finished. I approached Eddie and took the box from his outstretched hands. He glared at me. "We get a family discount, so I eat pizza a lot." Under my breath, I said to him, "play along."

"Like I have a choice," he hissed back.

"You'll have to eat that outside," Franny said. "The desk in the office is covered with paperwork, and I don't want the clothes to smell like pizza."

"Sure, we can do that," I said. "Follow me," I said to Eddie.

I carried the pizza down the hallway, out the back door, and rested the box on top of the HVAC unit. I could feel Eddie's energy winding up, so I spoke fast. "That's Franny. She's Ronnie Holiday's niece. I told her he hired me to do the store visual displays and she wanted me to start today."

"They offered me that job."

"They offered Eddie Adams that job. You're August July."

"I thought you were April May."

"I can't be the same person who sold her uncle the trunk! She might know about her. It's too suspicious, me turning up here asking questions. And I can't be me because I don't want anyone to know my real name. And you can't be you because I took your job. Besides, you work for the city. Why should you care if I take this job?"

"Visual work requires a specific skillset I'm not sure you have."

"Yes, but you're here now, so you can scan the store and give me ideas tonight so I can come back in the morning and pretend to know what I'm doing." I stood back and grinned. "Genius, right?"

Eddie grunted something that I took as a compliment. (I'm pretty sure he didn't intend it so.)

"You owe me," he said.

"I always owe you. Put it on my tab."

11

GLUE GUNS AND STRING LIGHTS

I ate two slices of pizza with Eddie, and then sent him on his way and returned to the store. Franny stacked the striped T-shirts on a pair of nested tables, lined up so the stripes flowed into each other. "Right now, I'm just getting this merchandise out," she explained. "If you want to make changes to the layout or the displays, take what you need. I can't wait to see the place after you bring it to life."

"Right," I said. "I'm going to have to think about it and come up with a concept."

"Sure, I get that," she said. She offered me a tight smile. "Just don't take too long. If we get any walk-in customers, I want them to be impressed."

"Ronnie said he had some ideas for the store. Would they be in his office?"

"If he had ideas, he didn't share them with me." She crossed her arms. "You never said where you met my uncle."

"At the—" I searched my brain. Where had I met him? Not the auction. "—restaurant next door. We met in the parking lot. I told him I'm a visual merchandiser, and he said you've been looking for someone for the store." I was on a roll. "I guess your other lead was the guy who does the visuals for the city of Ribbon, but he turned you down."

"That's who I wanted," she said. "I was impressed with what he did for the Pretzel Fest."

"He's not bad," I said, "if you go in for glue guns and string lights."

"You sound jealous."

I had to get her to stop talking about Eddie! "He's a workaholic. Regularly pulls all-nighters." Feeling a little bad about badmouthing Eddie, I added, "I hear he's good with paint removal."

She twisted her mouth to one side, pursing her lips in the process. She probably didn't know she did it, but her eyes dipped from my face to my T-shirt and skort and then down to my mom's Bernardo booties.

It wasn't a ridiculously Mod ensemble, but coupled with my red trench coat, which I'd worn in and set behind the counter, it did the job. Franny tipped her head to the side and then brought her assessing gaze back to my face.

"You're not exactly dressed for climbing on a ladder."

"I can be. I will be. I thought I'd spend the day going over Ronnie's notes." I finished, attempting for the second time to bring up the subject of Ronnie's files.

"We shared the office in the back, but it's mostly

invoices and delivery reports. With him gone, I'll be busy with deliveries and customers. I won't have time to babysit you."

"Of course. I'll start now."

"I've been here since six this morning and I'd like to call it quits soon. Fill out the paperwork I left on my desk and you can officially start tomorrow."

The shared office of Franny and Ronnie was about the size of a closet, and very well may have started life as one. Inside were two small white desks side by side. One held a laptop and other had a computer with a twenty-four-inch monitor. A bookcase was to the left of the left desk, the shelves covered in piles of invoices. Behind the desks was a poster for The Jam from a 1977 concert in Brighton, England.

There were two wheeled chairs behind the desk: one red, and one blue. I sat in the red one and leaned back. There seemed no doubt that this was, indeed, a shop dedicated to mod fashion, nor that the owners had a passion for the style. It was one thing to buy merchandise to assort the store, but to infuse the office with the same sensibility as the shopping space out front spoke to an authenticity that imitators overlooked. I was curious whether it was Franny or Ronnie who first had the idea and brought it to the other.

I was curious about a lot of things. Then again, I usually was.

Being back in a store had triggered me in a good way. Memories of my time working at Bentley's New York were buried in my mind. I'd advanced from selling shoes to buying them, eventually becoming the senior buyer of ladies' designer shoes. Along with traveling to see sample collections, writing orders, and strategizing for sales, I often stopped down to the selling floor and helped the manager merchandise before the store opened, or straightened displays on my lunch break. I regularly walked the rest of the store, too, to see what trends my colleagues had bought into (and to flex my employee discount.) (Would I get a discount? I hadn't even asked!) so I was more informed for my job.

All of that flooded back to me now. The excitement that comes from being around new clothes, the idea of discovering trends that crossed over clothing and shoes and sometimes even into housewares. Mixing and matching merchandise to tell a story. It was what Eddie did when he worked at Tradava, the now-defunct department store where we reconnected after I moved back to Ribbon.

I almost allowed the siren call of the store to distract me from my mission, which surprised me considerably, as there's not much that can tear my attention away from digging into someone else's business when the game's afoot.

The bookcase to the left of the desk was covered in neat stacks of paper. I picked up a few; they were unpaid invoices for merchandise. I replaced them and scanned the rest of the room. A black briefcase sat on one chair. I stuck my hand inside and pulled out an auction program. Inside, the listing for the trunk was circled and a notation in the margin said, "pick up from Samantha Kidd at the *Ribbon Eagle*" with yesterday's date.

That made no sense. How could Ronnie know who I was? Where I worked? That I was April May?

"Are you going through Uncle Ronnie's things?" Franny asked behind me.

Busted didn't describe the half of it. "Your uncle told me he had notes he wanted to share with me. I thought this was his briefcase, and I didn't want to bother you, so I thought—"

Franny snatched the briefcase out from under me, but not before my hand closed around a set of keys. I kept my fist balled up and shoved them deep into my pocket.

"You thought wrong." Her voice had gone cold. She pointed to a white folder with a blue, white, and red bullseye on the front. "Fill out the new hire paperwork and the W-9 for tax purposes. You can take the folder with you and bring back the signed forms tomorrow."

"Should we discuss a schedule?"

"Uncle Ronnie hired you, right? I assumed he went over everything with you." She seemed to reach the same conclusion I had. "I don't know what he offered to start you at, but until the store finds a customer base, I'd rather use you in a freelance manner."

"Sure, that makes sense."

I scooped up the folder and slid it into my handbag with the keys I'd just swiped, and then followed Franny out of the store. She locked the door behind me. I got into my car and drove away like everything was fine.

Somehow, I'd found myself smack in the middle of another mystery, and I could feel the kinetic energy that went along with that. Miscellaneous pieces of information, details that had come to me over the past few days, felt slightly out of reach, but they were there. It all started with the trunk.

My thoughts were interrupted by my phone. It was Eddie. "Yo," I answered.

"Dude, we're French."

"What?"

"The last name 'July.' Did you know it's pretty rare? Like three percent of the population has it. I looked up our history and it looks like it derived from the French word 'Juillet.' Do you think we're from France or Canada?"

"I think you're putting too much thought into it."

"I think Canada. I've always felt a connection to the Mounties."

As long as I had him on the phone... "Were you sincere in your offer to help me with my new job?"

"As I recall it wasn't so much an offer as an expectation."

"Good. Meet me at Senior's apartment for a key handoff."

"No can do. The graffiti artist moved to the mayor's house. I'm the person to call in case of cuss word emergencies."

"Can I bring them to you?"

"Sure."

I drove to the mayor's residence and found Eddie on

the sidewalk with a bucket of paint and a roller on a stick. He'd changed into a white T-shirt with a red maple leaf in the middle. Around the leaf, it said CANADA IS MY HAPPY PLACE.

The letters "-uck" were still visible on the sidewalk. I pointed to the partial word. "I don't suppose people were wishing him good luck, were they?"

"Let's just say he's probably not getting reelected."

I dropped the spare set of Mod Holiday keys into Eddie's outstretched palm, and he dropped them into one of the many pockets of his pants.

"You're safe between the hours of midnight and six," I said.

"That's when I do my best work."

I left Eddie to his neighborhood beautification project. The past twenty-four hours had left me unsettled. Maybe it was the presence of the trunk at The Mod Holiday, or maybe it was Ronnie's untimely death. All of this could be my active imagination and need to fabricate excitement in my life, but there was one question that loomed over the whole mess of it. Why did Ronnie Holiday drive into a tree?

At times like these, it's good to have friends in interesting places. I called the county coroner's office. Only one person answered the phone there, and that was the person I wanted to reach.

"Hi, Patti, it's Samantha Kidd."

"'Sup?" (Patti didn't mince words.)

"You wouldn't, um, have been tasked to do an autopsy this morning, were you?"

"That *is* the job of the coroner."

"Right. I'm not taking a survey. I—um—heard about a questionable death by—um—motor vehicle, and I—um—don't know if it was ruled—um..."

"Tell me what you need to know and cut out the um-um-um stuff."

"Last night, a man drove into a tree in the parking lot of The Pho. His name was Ronnie Holiday, and I had some business dealings with him."

"When were these business dealings?"

"A few hours before he died."

A stretch of silence passed before Patti spoke again. "Ronnie Holiday's body came in this morning. The cause of death appears to be head injury caused by a collision. A seat belt would have saved his life."

I loved having a competent friend in the morgue! I mean, it was nice to talk to someone who didn't second-guess my motives for asking about a recently deceased person. I didn't even have to waste time on small talk.

"That's your official word?"

"No, that's what the orderly at the hospital told me when he delivered the body. Open and shut case."

"Do you agree?"

"No, I don't. Ronnie Holiday's cocaine readings were off the charts. Either he time-traveled back to the eighties or someone slipped him a dose that proved fatal."

WOLVES IN SHEEP'S CLOTHING

"I've got about twenty minutes left on my break," Patti said. "Charlie's here too. Come by and we can talk about his in person."

"Charlie?"

"Charlie Loncar. You two know each other, right?"

I'd gone a long time not knowing the first name of Ribbon's lead homicide detective. He was, and would always be, Detective Loncar to me. But as his life shifted from the homicide beat for the city of Ribbon and my life shifted from murder suspect to someone who had a genuine interest in solving crimes, it was inevitable that we'd get to know each other on a whole other level. The times, they were a-changing.

"Why is Detective Loncar at the coroner's office?"

"I asked him to bring me lunch."

I checked the clock. It was a close to two. I was due at the paper in an hour, which meant I had a small window for a field trip to the morgue. If Monty knew I was chasing a story, he might give me a pass, but there was something suspicious about Monty's interest in the trunk too. I swung a U-turn at the next intersection and drove to the morgue.

I parked next to Detective Loncar's car. Thanks to my ill-advised suggestion that he get a sportscar to spiff up his image, we now drove matching Limited Edition Refraction Blue Toyota Supras. I'd gone from being embarrassed by our status as twinsies to embracing it. The presence of another car just like mine made mine stand out less, and with an eye toward going unnoticed, standing out less worked in my favor.

There were a few entrances to the morgue. One door opened onto a large, cavernous room with four desks positioned around the perimeter. This was where the detectives who served the county worked. The sheriff was the only member of the staff to have an office, which probably came in handy when shaking down the mayor for budgetary increases. (I'm just guessing.)

The second entrance was on the opposite side next to the docking station where vans from the ER delivered bodies. I left my car and walked to that side of the building, where I found Patti and Loncar sitting at a picnic table. A pink box of assorted donuts sat between them. There were seven left; two had colorful sprinkles.

"Hey, Sam," Patti said. She wore a white T-shirt over a black bra, and black, boxy trousers. A balled up apron sat on the picnic bench next to her.

"Hi," I said to her. "Hi, Detective," I added.

"Ms. Kidd," he replied.

Detective Loncar was a late sixties former homicide detective turned restless retiree turned private investigator. Two years ago, I'd facilitated a makeover with the help of Nick and his dad, and these days the detective dressed in a uniform of black blazer, white shirt, and dark Wranglers. The first time I'd ever encountered him, I interpreted the Wranglers as a poor fashion choice and an indicator of his investigative prowess. I've been known to judge people based on their clothes, which occasionally pans out but sometimes makes it easy for wolves who like to wear sheep's clothing.

My relationship with Detective Loncar was not the sort to require regular interactions, and that meant I usually only saw him when there'd been a crime. Even though elements of his style makeover had stuck, he was still intimidating in his own way. At one time, he had the power to arrest me; that's a difficult thing to forget.

"Ms. Detweiler asked me to bring her lunch," Loncar said. The fact that they used almost the identical explanation, offered before I had a chance to ask, tipped me off that it was a cover story. I let him believe I didn't doubt him, which would certainly work in my favor somewhere down the road.

"The paramedics declared Ronnie Holiday D.O.A.," Patti said. "They had no reason to think this was anything other than what it appeared to be. The victim had injuries consistent with a car accident. He wasn't wearing a seatbelt, and the front end of his car was mashed against a tree. I don't think this was negligence."

"You said his blood tests showed high cocaine levels. Is it common for the hospital to miss that?" I asked.

"Blood tests happen here. It's standard procedure for any autopsy. The first thing I do is to take blood samples and run four tests: carbon monoxide, cocaine, alcohol, and DNA. Most of the time they're standard readings. I log the victim's results onto the chart and file the samples. Mr. Holiday's cocaine was so high it registered in the fatal zone before I had a chance to write it down."

"Do you think this was an accidental overdose?"

"Difficult to say at this point. Why all the questions?"

"I saw him drive into the tree. Something didn't seem right." I shifted my gaze from her to Loncar. "I was there."

"Where?" Loncar asked.

"The Pho. It's an Irish-Vietnamese Fusion restaurant across the street from the Kirkville hotel. You know it, right? I was there with Nick. Ronnie called me. He said he knew what I did and then he drove into a tree."

"I'm confused," Patti said.

Loncar held his hand up. "Allow me. I have experience with her."

I flushed out my recollection for them. "I saw the accident from inside the restaurant," I explained to Patti. She nodded, as if that part she understood. "I thought I recognized Ronnie's car from earlier when he came to the newspaper offices. I honestly thought he followed me. He drove into the parking lot across the street and circled the building. When he left, his car weaved across the traffic as if he were drunk, and then he entered The Pho parking lot and drove into a tree. A woman—a neighbor of Senior's—was there, too. When I got to the car, she ushered me back into the building."

"Petra Moon?" Loncar asked.

"Yes. She owns the restaurant. Do you know her?"

"I met her husband Phil at a poker game."

In some ways, Ribbon was a small town. Detective Loncar first met Nick's dad through me, but the two of them hit it off in a way only bachelors over the age of sixty-five can. Senior tended to stir up trouble, and Loncar tended to tamp it down, resulting in a zero sum game of Life. Senior considered Loncar his wingman, and Loncar saw Senior as proof positive that life doesn't end at seventy. I suppose it could have been worse, but some days I couldn't figure out how.

"There's one small detail I haven't mentioned," I said.

"There always is," Loncar replied.

I looked at Patti and then back at Loncar. Since retirement, Loncar was a private citizen, but Patti was on the city's payroll and that came with obligations to follow protocols.

She seemed to recognize I wasn't comfortable floating theories around a city employee. "Tell you what. I'll do a full autopsy and see what else I find."

"How long will that take?"

"I won't know anything conclusive for the rest of the day. I'm on call tonight, so it might be tomorrow if something more pressing interrupts me. But if this wasn't an accident, I have to notify the authorities."

"Any chance you can notify me too? As a concerned citizen?"

"Sure," she said. "Mr. Holidays' cause of death will become a public record. Once the results are conclusive, you can print it in the paper for the whole city to read."

13

A MATCH MADE IN HEAVEN

PATTI STOOD. "MY BREAK IS OVER. YOU TWO STAY AS long as you want." She went back inside.

We both watched her walk away. "She likes you," I said. I sat back and held both hands up in a hands-off manner. "Don't ask me how I know. I can just tell. And don't pretend that doesn't mean anything. You know me well enough to know I can read people."

Loncar turned around and looked at the door where Patti had entered the building. "She's only five years older than my daughter."

"Yes, but you had your daughter when you were young."

"I had my daughter when I was thirty."

I flapped my hands. "None of that stuff matters. You're single. She's single. You both kind of work in the same field. It's a match made in heaven." I leaned forward and picked up a cruller. I took a bite. It tasted like cardboard. I set the other half down on a napkin.

"How did you know the deceased?" Loncar asked, making it clear he was done talking about his love life. I didn't mind much, since I can be like a dog with a bone and I knew we'd revisit the conversation in due time.

"I met him yesterday." It sometimes surprised me how much I could pack into a day. "I recently bought a trunk at auction, and he wanted it. He came to the newspaper and offered to buy it from me sight unseen."

"The Boyd Brighton auction?"

I sat back. "How did you know?"

"I've heard some buzz about it. Did you sell?"

"Yes." I stared at the donuts. "I don't think that was the right decision."

Loncar raised his eyebrows. "I can't help thinking there's a connection between Ronnie buying the trunk and Ronnie dying. It seems odd to buy something and then die before you get a chance to inspect it, you know?"

"What was it you wanted to tell me when Ms. Detweiler was here?"

"Ronnie didn't know my real name. I attended the auction under the name April May—it's a fake name I use as a byline for the paper. Ronnie came to the office and asked for April, so my editor told me to just answer to her name and not explain things. But he was on a phone call when he died, and the name on his screen was Samantha Kidd."

"How do you know that?"

I pulled Ronnie's phone out of my pocket and set it on the table between us. Loncar reached forward and took the phone. The screen showed images of turtles swimming in the ocean. "What's this?"

"It's a video of underwater life. Very relaxing. It's eleven hours long and the phone won't lock as long as it's playing." I added, "I turned the sound down so I wouldn't go into a trance."

Loncar tapped the screen and accessed the main menu, then scrolled through the recent calls. My name showed up a few times. "You only called him once?"

"Yes. To tell him I would sell him the trunk. But I called him from the paper. Carl Collins gave him my cell number."

Loncar tapped a few more buttons. "Mr. Holiday knew who you were." He held the phone up to show Ronnie's contacts. Samantha Kidd was listed as a primary contact, and underneath, in the notes field, was the name April May.

"Nobody knows I'm April May," I said.

"Nobody?" Loncar asked.

"My editor, my coworker, Nick, Eddie, and me."

"That's not nobody." Loncar set the phone back on the table. "There's another explanation."

"What?"

"Ronnie knew who you were before you introduced yourself."

It was looking that way, especially after finding his notes on the auction catalog. And of the possible sources, one troubled me more than the others. Monty had assigned the trunk story to me, and then he told me to meet with Ronnie. He instructed me to sell, but according to Carl, Monty lied about the paper needing Ronnie's money. For someone who dedicated his life to the news, Monty seemed to have something to hide.

"Tell me about this trunk," Loncar said.

"It was listed as a sealed trunk from the sixties," I said. "Nobody wanted it. The contents were unknown. I bought it for fifty dollars."

"How much did Mr. Holiday pay you for it?"

"Fifty thousand."

Loncar stared at me for a moment and then repeated the figure. "Fifty thousand dollars."

"Yes."

"For a sealed trunk."

"Yes."

"That you bought for fifty dollars."

"Yes."

"Did you look inside?"

"It was sealed."

"That's not what I asked."

There wasn't much reason to lie to Loncar. "Ronnie warned me not to look in the trunk. Not like *Raiders of the Lost Ark* warned, but like there was something inside he wanted and if I knew it was there, I might change my mind on selling."

"And?"

"I took a cigar box out of the trunk before I sealed it." I pulled the passports out of my bag and handed them to him. Loncar flipped them open one after the other.

"How old was this trunk?"

"Sealed since the sixties, at least that's what the auction catalog said."

Loncar handed the passports back to me. "Sixty year old intelligence isn't worth a lot to anyone."

"That's what I thought."

"Anything else you can tell me about the trunk?"

"We have an intern at the paper who manages our social media feeds. She took some pictures, which I can get when I go in for today's staff meeting."

"Where's this trunk now?"

"At Ronnie's store. I don't know how it got from Ronnie's car to the store, but I was working there when someone delivered it." Loncar raised his eyebrows questioningly.

"I thought you worked for the newspaper."

"I like to stay busy."

"Ms. Kidd, when did you start working at Mr. Holiday's store?"

"This morning."

"I don't suppose that was a lucky coincidence."

"Not exactly."

"When are you due back at your job?"

"The paper? I've got a staff meeting at three." I checked my phone. "Crap. I'm late."

I stood and Loncar put his arm out to stop me. "I want you to go back to your new job," he said. "Keep an eye on that trunk. Let me know if anybody suspicious shows up."

"You're asking me for help," I said. "Are you sure about this?" I asked.

"I'm starting to have my doubts." He waited a moment and then added, "Thank you for your cooperation, Ms. Kidd."

"You know you don't have to call me that anymore."

"Thank you for your cooperation, Ms. May."

————

I HAD SEVEN MINUTES TO GET TO THE PAPER. AT TIMES like these, it was handy to have a sports car. I made suitable time, cut off two truckers and only got the finger from one, and pulled into the *Ribbon Eagle* parking lot six minutes later. I ran up the stairs and burst into the office. Carl, Kristi, and Frank, our sports guy, sat in Monty's office. Monty looked at me through the glass partition and gestured for me to join them.

I went straight to the office. "Sorry I'm late."

Monty's coloring tended toward high-blood-pressure red, but today he was a pinkish shade. Like salmon before it's baked. A bottle of Pepto Bismol sat on his desk next to his phone. Pink phone messages were tucked under the corner of the bottle. For a tough newspaper editor, he had a lot of pink in his office.

"Geez, Kidd," Carl said. "Way to make us wait."

"I'm only three minutes late, and since when does Monty hold up a staff meeting for one person?"

"Since that person has the one story Monty cares about," Carl said. He pulled his straw hat off of his head and then repositioned it low over his forehead.

"Me? I write about fashion."

"Ronnie Holiday? The trunk from the mod auction? Does this ring any bells?" Carl said.

I looked from Carl to Monty. "I thought you killed the trunk story." I quickly glanced at Kristi, who was drawing daisies on her notepad, and Oswald, who appeared to be shooting people on a video game on his phone. "I told April she had to find another lead."

"April doesn't need a new story," Monty interrupted me. "I want you to work on the trunk article with her. You'll share a by-line. Special feature, six inches, color in the weekend supplement, and prime web placement."

"I took photos," Kristi piped up. She looked at me, and then at Monty. He nodded his approval. She smiled and went back to drawing daisies.

"Today's Wednesday," I said. "Don't you think it's rushing things to run this in the weekend supplement?"

"This is hot, and it's family-friendly. I gave Frank an extra two pages for high school sports coverage and I already expanded the letters to the editor. We added trivia to the games page and increased the size of photo of the week. I need pages, Kidd. Oswald's an ad-selling machine, but if we don't have pages, we can't sell ads. Use Kristi's pictures. Kristi, get Samantha your pictures and include her in—what do the kids call it when you make a big deal out of the packaging?"

"Unboxing."

"Right. Use the photos to tease the unboxing on our feeds."

I turned and looked at the door behind us that

separated us from the bullpen. "But we never unboxed it."

Monty leaned against the edge of his desk. "Interns. Out," Monty barked. Kristy and Oswald collected their things. Monty waited until the door shut behind Oswald to address the rest of us. "You too, Mazurkiewicz," he said to Frank.

Frank looked at me and Carl and then at Monty. "It's a good thing nobody dies on the sports page. You people would steal a story from your mother."

14

WHO'S YOUR SOURCE?

AFTER FRANK LEFT, IT WAS A MEETING OF FOUR: Monty, Carl, April, and me.

"What's going on?" I asked.

"I'll tell you what's going on," said Carl. "You're the luckiest person I know. You buy a trunk at auction, some guy shows up to buy it, and later that day he drives into a tree. It's like someone sprinkles fairy dust everywhere you go."

Monty crossed his arms. "Are you done?" he asked Carl. He twisted around, grabbed the pink messages from his desk, and held them out toward Carl. "These are the people who wanted the trunk. Find out who they are and why they wanted it. Dig up anything you can on Ronnie Holiday."

"Ronnie Holiday owns a mod boutique out on Duocacy Road. He was their creative director. He has one sister, who is currently on a twenty-one-day cruise outside of Miami. Her husband died five years ago from a terminal illness. There's a niece, Franny Holiday, who co-owned the store with Mr. Holiday. The trunk was delivered there this morning, and I might be able to access it again." Carl and Monty stared at me. "What?" I asked. "Just because you told me to kill the story doesn't mean I listened."

"Is your husband out of town again?" Carl asked.

"My husband supports my interest in journalism."

Carl snorted. "And your interest in murder?" he asked.

"Who said anything about murder? He drove into a tree."

Carl and Monty exchanged a look. Monty nodded and Carl turned to me. "I got a call from my contact at the coroner's office. Holiday's blood test raised some red flags. There's a strong possibility he was dead before the accident."

As far as I knew, Patti was the one who ran those blood tests and she wasn't going to have final autopsy results for a few hours. "Who's your source?" I asked.

"Nice try, Kidd," Carl said. He looked at Monty. "I cover crime. The story should be mine."

It figured Carl had already wormed his way into Patti's trust. I'd never once mentioned confidentiality in my conversation with her. Carl was the crime reporter; my job was style. I should have asked Patti about Ronnie Holiday's shoes.

Monty stood before us with his arms crossed. His bushy eyebrows were low over his eyes and his mouth turned down at the corners. Whatever he was gearing up to say was taking him a good minute to get out, which wasn't like him. Finally, he spoke. "This story stays with Samantha."

"What?!" Carl asked. He tossed his pen onto the notepad on his lap. It skidded off, landed on the floor, and rolled under Monty's desk. He dropped down to his hands and knees to fish it out and said, "She writes about neon yellow sweatshirts."

I was surprised Carl had paid that much attention to my articles. He wasn't wrong; my tongue-in-cheek piece about construction workers being on-trend had led to a run on neon sweatshirts at the local department store (which I learned after I went to buy one myself).

"Show me what you got, Kidd," Monty said. He pointed to the door. "Now both of you get out of my office."

Carl stayed behind in Monty's office after I left. I had a feeling as soon as he thought I was out of earshot; he'd start a campaign to make Monty miserable enough to change his mind.

But would he? Just yesterday, Monty told me to sell, said the paper needed money, and tried to divert my interest in the story. Today he wanted me back on it. It could be that I'd proven myself as a capable reporter or it could be something else. If Monty were hiding something that connected back to Ronnie, would he give the assignment to Carl, or would he give it to me?

I dismissed this last thought as paranoia. Monty had a way of treating everything that happened in Ribbon as if it were a Pulitzer Prize winning opportunity. I didn't know much about his background, but I knew at his core, he wanted what was best for the paper. Maybe that's what made me like this job more than any of the others I'd taken since moving back home. Besides, my story on hemlines was something.

I'd expected to show up at the newspaper, sit in on the staff meeting, and then head back to The Mod Holiday, but this new assignment changed my plans for the afternoon. I was antsy to get back to The Mod Holiday and get into that trunk, but now I had new motivation for staying. I flipped through the pink messages. Monty said these people were interested in the trunk like Ronnie had been. It was as good a place to start as any.

I scanned the bullpen. Open seating and cubicle-style workstations may have been good for productivity, but they were awful for privacy. There was only one private office we used when calls of a confidential nature were required. It was the old operator's booth. There were no windows and no circulation, which left it mostly unoccupied. Monty assigned it to Oswald when he came to work at the paper, something about paying his dues. I wondered a bit at Oswald's ad-selling success and if Monty had dangled the carrot of a desk in the bullpen with the rest of us.

I went to Oswald's office and tapped on the door. Today his bowtie and suspenders were green. "Can I use your office for an hour?" I asked.

Oswald shrugged. "Fine by me," he said. "It's hang-up-on-the-caller day." He kept his eyes glued to his phone and shot a couple more bad guys while he walked out. It was impressive how he didn't run into the doorframe.

Oswald had an open bag of experimental sesame pretzel sticks from Tom Sturgis sitting on his desk. Occasionally, one of the local pretzel companies would make a small batch of a new flavor, package them up and sell them in their gift shop. If the locals deemed it a hit, it would go into the regular line, and if not, it would go silently into the night. These were definitely worth adding to the line-up. I'd have to buy a dozen bags to help sway the powers that be in their decision.

I ate a handful of pretzel sticks, washed them down with coffee, and checked Ronnie's phone. Eight hours had passed on the fish video. I swiped up and accessed the call logs, then compared the numbers to the ones Monty gave me. There was one match. It seemed the smart place to start.

There was no answer. After four rings, a computer generated male voice repeated the number back to me and told me to leave a message. I hung up.

The first call was the auction house. "Hi," I said. "This is—" I stopped for a second. April May had originally bought the trunk so her name might raise questions. "Samantha Kidd from the *Ribbon Eagle*. I'm returning a call made about a trunk purchased at the Boyd Brighton auction."

"Yeah, that was me. Our records show an April May as the buyer. She listed the paper as her contact number."

"That's correct. She works with me."

"Is she there?"

"She's on a call at the moment, but anything you want to say to her, you can say to me." I was getting surprisingly good at covering my tracks. "She bought the trunk on behalf of the newspaper, so it's not hers, per se."

"Per se? Right. Listen. We had a data breach a few nights ago, and April May's name was exposed. Our tech team has since put a patch into the system, but it's my job to contact the victims and let them know."

Suddenly, the office felt cold. "What information was leaked?"

"Names, contact information, record of sale."

"That's everything!"

"Not everything. The system blocks the amount of each bid and the payment method. Your colleague was smart to use the newspaper as her address. It could have been a lot worse. You'll give her the message?"

"Consider it done."

I hung up and made notes. I had a strong suspicion Ronnie was behind the data breach. From the moment he walked into the newspaper office with his fifty thousand dollar bid, I'd wondered how he knew I (April) bought it. This explained a lot.

Was the trunk the only thing Ronnie wanted from the auction? If so, why did he want it? Unless he had X-ray vision, how could he know what was inside?

It also raised more questions. Was Ronnie a collector who tried to buy up everything sold at the Boyd

Brighton Auction? Why? Was he shopping on behalf of his new store, or was this a personal obsession? Did Franny know anything about his pursuit?

The next three numbers resulted in a voicemail on the first, a hang-up on the second, and a renewed subscription on the third after learning she was a fan of my column. I snuck in a call to Nick, but he didn't answer. It was almost six, and the only thing I'd eaten all day were half a bag of experimental sesame pretzel sticks (you didn't really think I stopped at a handful, did you?) and a bagel sandwich. And two pieces of pizza and half a donut. Huh. Maybe that's why my skort was tight. It's a good thing I stay active.

I gathered Ronnie's phone and my notepad and left. The office was quiet. Oswald was in a chair by the windows. He held his phone in both hands and tapped at the screen with his thumbs. "You can have your office back," I said.

He looked up. "Keep it," he said, and then set his phone on the desk in front of him. "That phone is cursed. People see the word 'subscriptions' and screen the calls."

"I thought the phones all said '*Ribbon Eagle*.'"

"All but that one. Something about not misleading the public."

"So hang-ups and no-answers might be because people think I'm trying to sell them something?"

"Right." He glanced at the laptop in front of him. "I renewed nineteen people since you went in there. One more and Monty owes me a bonus."

I tore a page out of my notepad and handed it to Oswald. "Congratulations."

"Sweet!" He typed the information into his spreadsheet and shut down the computer. "Are you leaving?"

"In a minute. I'm going to make a call from out here."

"Smart." Oswald shoved his phone into the back pocket of his jeans and left.

The light coming through the exterior windows was minimal compared to earlier. As the sun set behind the community college, the sky turned the color of an orange creamsicle. It would be dark in an hour.

I went to my desk and punched in the first number I'd called. Four rings, and then the computer generated voice. I'd already left one message, so I hung up. I pulled Ronnie's phone out of my pocket and restarted the fish video, then double checked the call logs. This number was all over them.

Before I thought through my next impulse, I touched the number. Immediately, the phone started to ring. I was alone in the office, so I put the call on speaker. A female voice answered on the first ring.

"Who is this?" she demanded. "Why do you keep calling me? I told you I haven't seen that trunk for sixty years. Please, just leave me alone."

15

BARELY HAD TO LIE

"Hello," I said. "This is —" be smart about this, Samantha — "April May," I said. "I bought a trunk from the estate of Boyd Brighton. Are you the original owner?"

"How did you get this number?" the woman asked.

"You called the *Ribbon Eagle*," I said. "My editor gave me a message to call you back." Being both Samantha Kidd and April May was turning out to be ridiculously easy. I barely had to lie!

"Where did you get the number you're calling me from?"

Oh. Right. This was Ronnie Holiday's phone. Crap. "This phone belongs to Ronnie Holiday."

"He approached me about buying the trunk."

Attempting to stick to the truth was turning this into a fruitless conversation. I still knew nothing about the woman on the other end of the phone aside from the fact that Ronnie had pursued her relentlessly prior to his death. I couldn't even tell if she knew he died, which meant either she was still in the dark or she was as good a liar as I was.

"Ronnie Holiday was in a fatal car accident yesterday. I honestly don't know why he wanted the trunk. Can we meet to talk about this?"

There was a stretch of silence on the other end of the phone. Face to face, I could have gauged her reaction, but I was out of luck. "Come to the Kirkville Hotel. Ask for Beatriz."

"Is that you?"

"Yes. I get a break at nine."

The Kirkville Hotel wasn't a hotel—at least not anymore. It was a restaurant known for two things: their burger menu, and their rough clientele. I'd eaten there on occasion, usually during the day, and always with a friend. All things considered, it was time to call in a professional.

———

I WENT HOME TO CHANGE AND CHECK ON LOGAN. HE sat right inside the front door. He meowed his hello, and then turned around and led me to the kitchen. I replenished his food and water bowls and then watched him turn up his nose at his regular fare. "Fine," I said. I pulled a pint of Turkey Hill vanilla ice cream from the freezer and gave him a scoop. "Don't tell your father." He meowed and immediately got ice cream all over his whiskers.

Upstairs, I pulled a blue and white striped sweater over my white T-shirt, pulled my red trench coat over the sweater, and left.

I drove to the Kenhorst Plaza, which was the opposite direction of the Kirkville Hotel. Detective Loncar retired right around when his wife divorced him after a zillion years of marriage, and too much free time on his hands had led him to open the PI business. I didn't know if he maintained an active case load or if the office was just a place for him to play Solitaire during the day.

Loncar's car was in a space out front. Instead of calling attention to our matching cars, I drove to the side of the building and parked under a tree.

There were two things I expected when I went to visit Loncar, and my expectations were almost always satisfied. First, he'd be there. Second, he'd be alone. On a few occasions, his daughter brought her kids and sat behind the reception desk, giving the appearance that he had staff. After her second baby, he discouraged the visits. Something about the playpen in the corner sending the wrong message to prospective clients.

Loncar was making coffee. "Ms. Kidd," he said when I entered.

"Mr. Loncar," I said back.

I dropped into the chair across from him even though he stood. "I'm here to hire you."

He stared at me. I stood and tucked on leg underneath me and then sat back down. "I have a lead on the original owner of the trunk. She wants me to meet her at the Kirkville Hotel and I don't want to go by myself."

"Where's your husband?"

"Italy." I stood up and unfolded my leg and sat back down. Loncar needed more comfortable chairs. "Look. I'm trying to learn from my mistakes. What's your rate?"

"One fifty an hour billed against a two thousand dollar retailer. Plus expenses."

I reached into my handbag and tore open the envelope of cash Ronnie Holiday had left at the paper in exchange for the trunk. I pulled out a chunk of bills and slapped them down on the table.

He glanced at it. "I don't want that money," Loncar said.

"Why not? Isn't it good enough for you?"

"It's pink." I looked down at the cash. The stack of bills on Loncar's desk were the color of strawberry ice cream. Either Ronnie had paid me in counterfeit cash or Carl was back to his April Fools shenanigans. I picked up a bill and saw Carl's smiling face beaming out from the center. Curses!

"I'll pay you in real money," I said, while sliding the pink bills back toward my handbag. "I didn't know these were fake."

"Don't be too hard on yourself. Identifying counterfeit bills requires certain observational skills."

"Now you're just patronizing me."

Loncar leaned back in his chair. "Tell me about this meeting."

I filled the detective in on how I came to talk to

Beatriz after finding her number on both the messages at the paper and Ronnie's phone. "I said I wanted to meet her to discuss the trunk and she told me to come to the Kirkville. I'm supposed to be there in," I checked the time on my phone, "twenty minutes."

"Do you carry pepper spray?"

"You'd think I would by now," I said, "but no."

The detective opened a drawer and pulled out a small canister. "If you use it, make sure it's pointed away from you." He pushed the cannister toward me. "Keep it handy and try not to let anybody know you have it." I took the can and slipped it into my coat pocket. I felt invincible.

The good thing about partnering with Loncar was that I was almost entirely certain he wouldn't let me do anything illegal or stupid.

I waited out front while Loncar locked his office. "So...rock paper scissors on who drives?" I asked. I made a fist, then straightened out my fingers, then pantomimed scissors.

Loncar glared at me. "I'll give you a head start. Park at the hotel. I'll park behind The Pho."

"No. Park behind The Mod Holiday. No one will question the car. They'll think it's mine."

The sun had disappeared behind the horizon. Salmon stripes stretched across an otherwise dark blue sky, interrupted occasionally by puffs of cumulous clouds moving at a dangerous pace. I hoped it wasn't a sign.

Any residual rush hour traffic was long gone, and the roads were mostly clear. The closer I got to the agreed upon destination, the more motorcycles I noticed on the road. By the time I reached the hotel, the front lot was full of them. Like someone had turned on an *Easy Rider* homing device. I drove past the bikers and circled the lot until I found a space.

I called Loncar. "The eagle has landed," I said. Loncar didn't say anything. I checked the screen. "Hello? Are you there?"

"Turn up your volume and put your phone in the pocket closest to your face. Don't pull your phone out in front of anybody. Try to bring up Ronnie Holiday. Repeat anything you want me to hear."

It wasn't lost on me that Loncar was giving me instruction, and instead of making a mess of the evening, I wanted to do this right. I wanted him to trust me.

"Got it," I said. I bent my head down and checked for pockets. The coat was heavy cotton sateen that had been treated with a water repellant, and that made it somewhat stiff and cumbersome. The pockets were on a diagonal above the drawstring waist. They had flap closures that snapped shut. I unsnapped the one on the left and was about to put the phone into it when I heard Loncar's voice again.

"Ms. Kidd," he said.

I put the phone back to my head. "Yes?"

"You're a smart, engaging woman. Get people talking and pay attention to what they say and what they don't. Try not to say anything you heard on *the Mod Squad.*"

Just when I thought he was being nice!

"I'm hanging up now." I disconnected, and then realized what I'd done. I immediately called him back. "I'm new at having a partner."

"I know."

If I said good-bye, chances were I'd hang up again, so I dropped my phone into my pocket, grabbed my handbag, and headed inside.

There were two entrances: one by the porch where the leather-clad loiterers stood in clumps, and one on the opposite side that entered onto the dining room. Beatriz hadn't specified where to find her, so I went with the safe, family-friendly gamble and walked around to the dining room side. An Eddie Cochran song floated out of the doors, getting louder or softer each time the doors opened or closed. I yanked on the door and a young man in a black T-shirt and jeans greeted me.

"How many?" he asked, grabbing menus.

I held up my hands. "I'm not here to eat. I'm looking for Beatriz," I said.

He pointed to the hallway. "She's tending bar."

So much for the safe family-friendly gamble.

I walked through the dining room and entered the bar. The room was a study in wood and vintage beer signs. Two bartenders worked from a center position, surrounded by bar top on four sides. One was a man with arms covered in tattoos. The other was a mature, willowy woman with wispy ash-blond hair partially secured in a low ponytail. She had a purplish bruise on her cheekbone and her lower lip was recovering from a split.

The woman set a foamy beer in front of a patron, wiped her hands on the napkin half tucked into her waistband, and gestured me closer. "What can I get ya?"

"I'm here to see Beatriz." I asked.

"I'm Beatriz. Who are you?"

"April May. I called earlier about the trunk."

She pointed to my handbag. "Let me see some ID."

Hmm. This could be a problem.

16

A REGULAR?

I<small>T WASN'T THAT</small> I <small>LOOKED UNDERAGE.</small> W<small>HICH MEANT</small>
Beatriz was already suspicious of me—for good reason. I
could A) run, B) refuse, or C) show her my Samantha
Kidd identification and try to explain. Blowing my cover
at the paper was the least of my concerns.

I reached for my wallet. My hands shook. I
unsnapped it and slid my license out of the sleeve when
a man in a baseball hat walked in. He held up his hand
and waved. "Yo, April. Sorry I'm late."

I have never been so happy to see Detective Loncar
in my life.

He'd changed from his black blazer and white shirt
into a faded chambray shirt with white snaps down the
front, jeans, and cowboy boots. The baseball hat kept
most of his face in shadow. I waved back. "Hey."

Beatriz pointed back and forth between us. "You
know her?" she asked him.

"Sure. She does some clerical work for me."

I stood back and stared at Loncar. Was he a regular here? How did he know Beatriz? Was Loncar secretly a biker? I glanced down at his cowboy boots. If Loncar were a biker, he'd choose different footwear.

Beatriz nodded at Loncar and then at me. "Come this way."

"We'll be right back," I said to the detective. "Female stuff."

He adjusted his baseball cap and nodded once. "I'll wait at the bar."

My first response at seeing Loncar was relief. This felt like a hostile environment, and now I was no longer alone. But by coming inside, he sacrificed his anonymity. I didn't know if they knew him but judging from the looks he got on his way to a barstool, they'd know him before he left.

Beatriz led me out of the bar to an empty room. A balustrade kept people from wandering inside. She moved the barrier and I passed though, and then followed her to a set of velvet club chairs that had seen better days. Faded and peeling wallpaper hinted at a more festive and welcoming environment.

"How did you find me?" she asked.

My presence here was the result of a string of lies, but this felt like time for the truth. "I bought a trunk at the Boyd Brighton auction. There's been a lot of interest in the trunk ever since it was delivered to me at the newspaper office, so I wanted to know more about it. I got your number from Ronnie Holiday."

What? It was the truth. Every last word. Sometimes I think I have a gift.

"The trunk was mine," Beatriz said. "I can't believe he had it all these years."

"Who?"

"Boyd. I was with Boyd in the sixties. We met when he was in the Modifiers."

"That had to be exciting," I said.

"Being in Boyd's orbit was something. I was a mod back then."

"I thought once a mod always a mod."

"For some people. That's not how it felt to me." She stared off, lost in the memory. "Boyd and I were part of the scene, right in the thick of it all. I can still remember how it felt when we walked into a room together. We tried to make a go of it, but things ended poorly. Secrets...that's what kills a thing, isn't it?" She looked away. "I—I made mistakes. We both did. After Boyd quit music, he became withdrawn and wanted to go out less and less. I was a party girl. London was swinging and the world was ours for the taking. I didn't understand him wanting to give it all up."

"Did you break up?"

"Not right away. Boyd started going out by himself. He had friends I never knew. I tried to understand him. I got into meditation. I thought if I could just understand what was going on in his mind, maybe I could pull us together. It didn't work." She looked down at her hands and balled them up together in her lap. "After Boyd and I split, I drifted. Connected to nothing.

I moved to California and spent some time finding my center. I stated reading self-help and spent a couple of years working in a natural food restaurant. The universe told me to keep moving, so I migrated east."

It was like looking at the ghost of Christmas Future. Sitting here with Beatriz, listening to her talk about her past, how she'd searched for something that made her feel connected and turned to new age methods to understand her world, it was familiar. I very clearly saw who I would be if I didn't learn how to live my life, mistakes, risks, failures, and all. I was on her path. For the past several years I had been searching for something just like Beatriz claimed to have done, but coming from her, it sounded like moon beams and gibberish.

"Did you ever talk to Boyd again?"

"No. I put that life behind me. I didn't even know that trunk still existed until someone contacted me about the auction. You don't still have it do you?"

I was prepared for the question. Not just prepared. Eager for it. Too many people wanted the trunk for me to assume Beatriz wouldn't.

"No," I said. "I sold it to Ronnie." I leaned forward and studied her. "That's why he was trying to reach you, wasn't it? He knew it was yours."

She nodded. "When the trunk showed up at the auction with the rest of Boyd's estate, historians wanted to establish the ownership so they could value it. The trunk had a luggage tag with my name on it."

"There was no luggage tag," I said. "The program

didn't mention you at all. The catalog said the trunk belonged to an unknown woman. If they knew it belonged to you, or even to the girlfriend of Boyd Brighton, why wouldn't they publicize that?"

"They probably would have if the tag didn't go missing."

Beatriz leaned back in her chair and ran her tongue over the split in her lip. She didn't seem nervous, shy, or scared. She seemed confident. Her energy had completely shifted from mere minutes ago when she was talking about her life with Boyd, and I found myself wondering which Beatriz was the real one?

"How did that happen?" I asked. I gestured to my face to indicate hers.

"There was an altercation at the bar a few nights ago. I had to break it up."

"Don't you have bouncers for that?"

"This isn't a nightclub, honey."

"What happened?"

"New guy came in asking a lot of questions. One of the regulars didn't like it." She gave the statement space. It hung in the air, a close description of what I was doing here tonight. "We're protective of ourselves here. It's like a family. When an outsider threatens that family, we handle it."

The energy in the room shifted. At first, Beatriz had been demure, portraying herself as a somewhat tragic figure. But as she spoke, she shed the cloak of sympathy. This felt like a threat.

I wasn't in the mood to be threatened. Loncar's

presence emboldened me. My phone was in my pocket, transmitting the whole conversation. If he thought I was in danger, he'd do something, so I pressed the issue.

"Ronnie Holiday is dead," I said. "His body is at the county morgue and the coroner will have the results of his autopsy in the morning. If there's anything suspicious about his death, and I suspect there will be, they're going to open a homicide investigation. Do you know what it's like to be part of a homicide investigation, Beatriz?"

She cocked her head slightly and her mouth gaped open. The bruise on her cheekbone and the split in her lip made her look tough, but her hands tightened around each other in her lap. She didn't say a word.

"I'll take that as a no," I said. I leaned forward. "Here's how it'll go: they'll try to establish the twenty-four hours prior to Ronnie's death. They'll talk to everyone he talked to and build a picture of where he had been and what he had done. They'll make note of any—" I paused for emphasis — "altercations he might have been involved in that could have escalated to violence." Now, I sat back in my chair. "Ronnie Holiday was part owner of the store across the street. I watched him drive through your parking lot the night he died. He paid good money for a trunk that belonged to you, and he died before he was able to access the contents. You might want to remember what it felt like to be in the thick of it all, because the way things look, you're going to be on their radar."

I said it to get a reaction. I wanted Beatriz to show

me fear or bravado—either would have told me she knew more than she indicated. But her eyes moved above my head and then back to me, and I sensed we were no longer alone.

"That's enough," said a male voice. I turned. A man the size of a small Mack truck filled the doorway. "It's time for you to leave."

17

JUST BEING FRIENDLY

THE MAN'S FACE WAS POCKMARKED AND ROUGH. A scar ran down one cheek and disappeared under his jawline. He was almost as tall as the doorframe and was solid muscle. "Get out," he said.

"We're not done with our conversation," I said.

"Yes, we are," Beatriz said. She looked at the man and nodded slightly.

"I'll handle this," he said. "You're needed out front."

She stood up. "Thanks."

Beatriz left me in the small, shabby-chic room with the Tasmanian devil. I stood too and held my hands up. "There's nothing to handle," I said. "We were just talking."

"Your conversation is over. Get out. And take your friend."

"What friend?"

"The one out front listening in on your conversation. He could use some company. Especially since he lost his phone." He pulled Loncar's phone out of his pocket. There was a live call in progress and my number was on the screen. Before I knew what was happening, the thug reached his fat fist into the pocket of my trench coat and pulled out my phone. "Would you look at that?" he said, holding the screens next to each other.

I reached out for the phones but the biker dropped them. They clattered to the uneven wooden floor. He brought the heel of his boot down on first Loncar's screen then mine. Each one shattered. "Go check on your friend before it's too late."

I went from competent reporter to scared enough to pee my pants faster than my car accelerates at a green light. "What did you do to him?"

He grinned. "We're just being friendly. Showing him a good time. Come out front and we'll show you a good time too."

Being here, talking to Beatriz, this whole night had been a bad idea. I'd tried to be smart by asking for Loncar's help, but I'd just dragged us both into trouble.

The biker released his grip on me and left the room. I followed him. My adrenaline levels were off the chart, and I could have overturned a school bus on my way to Loncar.

Except there was no school bus in my way. Loncar was at the bar in the same seat where I'd left him. His baseball hat was backwards and his eyes were bloodshot. In front of him sat five empty shot glasses and a full glass of beer. He looked up at me and squinted. "You wanna drink?" he slurred.

They'd gotten him drunk!

"No. I want to leave."

"M'kay. Lemme pay." He stood up and stumbled back a few steps, then raised his hands and got his balance. He pulled his wallet out and thumbed through his bills.

"I got it," I said. I removed a counterfeit pink hundred out of my handbag and set the full beer on top of Carl's smiling face. "Let's get out of here. Now."

Loncar nodded. He shuffled to the door with me behind him. A few people snickered, but mostly the crowd acted like this wasn't unusual, for which I was thankful. When we reached the door, the thug who broke our phones stood on the other side.

"Leaving so soon?" he asked.

Loncar swayed next to us. I grabbed his wrist and draped his arm around my shoulders to hold him up. His weight was staggering.

"Nice customer service around here," I said. "I'll mention it in my Yelp review."

He turned his head and spat. "Mind your business," he said. "Get your friend out of here and don't come back. Wouldn't want anything to happen."

"Is that a threat?"

"It's a warning. Leave Beatriz alone."

My fight or flight reflex wanted me to drop Loncar, run to the car, and drive as far away as possible. But since that was out of the question, I stumbled forward under his weight and headed to my car. The number of men in black leather loitering by the front door had dropped since I arrived, but still, it was enough to make me nervous.

The doors unlocked as I got close to the car. I opened the passenger side and Loncar collapsed inside. I looked back at the porch; a group of rough-looking customers appeared to have a laugh at someone's expense. The man with the gnarly disposition kept his eyes on us with no trace of amusement on his face.

Great. There was the not-so-small problem of leaving Loncar's car behind The Mod Holiday, but the truth was if I were being watched by thugs, I didn't want them to know I'd be back. Especially not now that I knew the trunk was inside the store. The trunk, connected to Ronnie, now had tentacles into Beatriz too. I wanted a second chance to look inside.

I drove to a residential neighborhood about half a mile away with Loncar snoring in the passenger seat. I parked next to the curb. I needed help, but my phone was broken. Loncar's phone was broken. Ronnie Holiday's battery was at seventeen percent. It had thirty minutes left on the fish video.

My phone had made me inherently lazy. I'd committed three numbers to memory and one of them was mine. Nick was in Italy. I called Eddie. "Hey," I said when he answered. "Any chance you're free?"

"If by 'free' you mean 'on my way to the mod shop to do your fake job for you,' then yes, I'm free."

"Listen carefully. Detective Loncar's car is behind the store, and he's with me. He's—" I leaned forward and looked at him. His mouth was partially open and his snoring had turned into soft breathing. "—asleep."

"You slept with Detective Loncar?"

"No!" I said. "It's a long story. Since you're already on your way, can you help me?"

"No can do. A, I've got a limited window of time to complete favor number one for you. Secondly, favor number two sounds like it involves the detective's car, and I need my car to maintain my gainful employment by the city."

There weren't many arguments against Eddie's valid points. I'd long ago maxxed out my credit on his favors. If I hadn't gone out on a limb for him in high school, we might never be even.

"Do you have the keys to the store?"

"I wasn't planning on breaking a window for access."

"Great. I'll be there when I can."

I hung up and restarted the fish video. Ronnie's call logs were full of numbers he'd called, but none of them helped me now. I glanced at Loncar again and thought of one person who might be willing to help.

I called information and got the number for the county coroner. Patti picked up on the third ring. "Coroner's office," she said.

"Patti, it's Samantha Kidd."

"Hey, Sam. 'Sup?"

"I need your help. I'm with the detective and ..." My voice trailed off. How do I say this? "He's too drunk to drive."

"You and Charlie party together? I didn't see that coming."

"No! No. We were on a job, see? Undercover. But they made him. They plied him with drinks. Things went south pretty quickly so I had to get him out of there."

"You're a riot," she said. I wished it were a joke. "What do you need from me?"

"You know how he and I drive the same car?"

"Yes."

"His is parked behind The Mod Holiday out on Duocacy Road. We were at the Kirkville Hotel, and the people who did this saw us drive away. I don't think it's wise to have a car just like mine in the neighborhood if you catch my drift. Can you help?"

"Sure. Where are you?" I gave her the cross streets. "Be there in twenty minutes."

18

SOUNDS LIKE A FUN TIME

WHILE I WAITED FOR PATTI TO ARRIVE, I THOUGHT back over my conversation with Beatriz. The biggest takeaway was that she'd been the original owner of the trunk. She claimed she didn't know what was in there, but I hadn't yet decided if I believed her.

By the time Patti arrived, Loncar was resting his head against the window and snoring quietly. Patti rapped her knuckles on my window and I unfastened my seatbelt and got out. "Thanks for this," I said.

She shrugged. "Sounds like a fun time." She wore a jean jacket over a black T-shirt, skinny black leather pants, and boots with a Cuban heel. Her hair was messy in a way that could have been intentional. I admired her ability to look like she either just rolled out of bed or came from the salon.

"Is there any news on the autopsy?"

"So far, nothing. There was a shootout in center city and four bodies came in last night. Since nobody's looking for details on Holiday except you guys, he went back into a locker."

"Sure," I said. "Just thought I'd ask."

"How do you want to move him?"

"It's almost a shame to wake him, but I don't think we can move him otherwise."

"We could leave him for now," she said.

"Sleeping of his buzz in a residential neighborhood? Waking up in a car that looks like his but isn't? I don't think that's a viable option."

"No. I'll drive your car. You can park mine behind the mod shop and take his. Mine's a junker. It's okay."

It was a convoluted solution to our problem but it solved a number of issues, not the least of which was not having to wake the sleeping detective.

Most people are attached to their cars. I wasn't. For twenty years, I drove a Honda del Sol that spent most of the time parked in a paid lot in New York City and eventually got destroyed by an opportunistic thug. I had a taxi driver on speed dial and begged rides from Nick and Eddie while I decided what to buy next. I even appropriated the vehicle of a murder suspect once. I am nothing if not resourceful.

"Okay. I'll call you tomorrow to coordinate getting your car." I peeked at Loncar through the window. "There's one more problem. I don't know where he lives."

"We could check his license."

"That requires us to access his wallet." I had an idea. I pulled Senior's keys out of my handbag. "Take him to my father-in-law's apartment. He's out of town so it's empty. Loncar's been there before so he already knows the place. I'll swing by in the morning."

I removed the car keys from my keyring and gave them to Patti, along with Senior's apartment number. I stood back on the sidewalk and watched her drive away in my car. It was late. It had been a long day, but after the night at the Kirkville hotel, I had a more pressing issue: getting back into that trunk. If I'd missed something the first time I was in it, I wanted to know.

The trunk was inside the store, buried under a stack of scooter helmets. I wanted a chance to go through it before it was too late. It was like *Charade*, when Audrey Hepburn and Cary Grant go through a flight bag, staring at everyday items to determine which one is a clue. If I left it there, Franny might open it or sell it to the next interested party and I'd never see it again.

I returned to The Mod Holiday and drove around the back. Loncar's blue Supra was the only car in the lot. The building was dark, illuminated by lights from The Pho next door. The music coming from the Kirkville Hotel across the street had shifted to early rockabilly, loud and raucous, and the patrons spilled onto the porch.

I circled through the lot and parked at The Pho. Chairs were stacked on top of tables, but the lights were still on. Phil, Petra's husband, saw me get out of my car and waved. He gestured me to the door and unlocked it and I entered.

"Hey, Sam," he said. "Twice in one week," Phil said as a greeting. "We must be doing something right."

"You are. Your colcannon noodle dish is amazing."

"I'd offer to make you some, but I already cleaned the kitchen. Want a bubble beer instead?"

In running a restaurant that mashed up two disparate food cultures, Phil and Petra had fused every conceivable dish. Some worked, some did not. A surprise was the Irish boba, a mix of Guinness and tapioca pearls. Phil told me once he made it on a dare and it's been on the menu ever since.

"No, that's not necessary," I said. I pointed my thumb over my shoulder. "I'm helping Eddie merchandise the store next door."

"I thought I saw your car over there earlier."

"I saw the lights on and stopped in. Is Petra here?"

Phil's face fell. He shook his head. "She hasn't been feeling well lately. Today's our slowest day of the week, so I told her to stay home."

I leaned against the counter. "She seemed fine when I talked to her this morning. I hope it wasn't the green bread."

Phil punched a couple of keys on the cash register and the drawer popped open. He pulled out the till and carried it to an open safe sitting along the far wall, slid the till inside, and closed the safe. He stood straight and turned to me. "To tell you the truth, she seemed fine to me too. Her temperature was normal and her insulin level was steady."

"I didn't know Petra was diabetic."

"Yes. She has it under control with medication, but some days, especially when we do a test kitchen, she spikes. When she said she didn't feel well I thought maybe it was something from the restaurant, but she said it wasn't food related." He shook his head. "Something's up with her."

"Since when?"

"Since the owner of the store next door came in the other day." He jutted his chin toward the mod shop. "She acted like she saw a ghost."

I didn't say anything because I knew exactly who he was talking about. Phil wasn't here the night Ronnie drove into the tree, so he might not know that I was. Petra had been here, though, and —what had she said? "You've seen what he's seen." It struck me as an odd thing to say at the time, but with everything else that had happened, I'd forgotten all about it.

"What made you and Petra decide to open The Pho in this location?"

"Petra found it. When we first started looking for a location she put out feelers with several commercial realtors in town. One of her leads contacted her about this property. It's privately owned by a group of investors. Most property owners would rather have an empty storefront with a high rent than lock someone in at a low one, but this group was described as highly motivated. The rent here is a third what it is on Penn Avenue."

"Did you consider how hard it would be to get customers?"

Phil shrugged. "It hasn't been easy. It was stroke of luck when The Mod Holiday moved in next door. We both have mod themes and attract a similar clientele. If we could do something about the biker bar across the street, we'd be in heaven."

"Maybe you should approach them about a reenactment of the Mods and Rockers 1964 Battle of Brighton," I suggested. "Like World War II weekend."

"Maybe we should." A pair of headlights flickered over the window. "Looks like Eddie is back."

I spun toward the window. Eddie's VW bug parked next to Loncar's Supra. He glanced at the car, looked around the parking lot, and then let himself into the store.

"That's my cue," I told Phil. "Thanks for keeping me company. Tell Petra I hope she feels better."

I left The Pho and walked across the parking lot. The back door to The Mod Holiday was propped open with a concrete block. I followed a thin light that lit the hallway into the main portion of the store. Eddie was struggling to move fixtures. I grabbed the opposite side of a chrome rounder and helped him walk it away from the wall.

"Whose car is that out back?" he asked.

"Patti Detweiler."

Eddie looked over his shoulder. "Is she here too?"

"She's with Loncar. I came back to get his car."

"You should run for mayor. Pretty soon you'll have the whole city working for you."

"No thanks, I'm not a fan of graffiti."

Eddie picked up some garments that had fallen from the rack and set them on top of the fixture. "I stopped off earlier to get a feel for the place. That wall was begging for a mural. I sketched it out and then left to get paint. It should be dry in the morning."

"About that. I can stay and help," I offered.

"You'll just be in my way. Go home and get some sleep. You're not twenty-five anymore."

"Neither are you," I reminded him. Eddie and I were the same age, which meant digs about me getting older reflected a lack of self-awareness on his part.

"Yes, but I slept until eleven, eat a macrobiotic diet, and my day didn't involve a drunk detective."

"Franny will be here by nine. You need to be gone by then."

"Dude, I'll be gone before it's light out. Four, maybe five. That's when I start to peak."

While I was inside the store with no known authority figures watching my every move, I had an opportunity to get into the trunk. I used the flashlight app from my phone to cut a path to it and unlocked the padlock with the combination Monty had given me. As I lifted the lid of the trunk, Eddie joined me and aimed both of our cell phone flashlights at the contents.

"Is everything there?" Eddie asked.

"Looks it," I said.

"Good. I'll help you carry it to your car."

I looked up at Eddie. In the darkness, with only the glow of the cell phone lights illuminating his face from below, he reminded me of the video for "Bohemian Rhapsody."

"I can't take it to my house."

"Why not? Nick's out of the country. You've got the whole house to yourself. It's like the old days."

"Franny saw the trunk arrive. Even if she doesn't care about it, she'll notice if it's gone. Especially since her recently deceased uncle bought it. She's cold and unemotional now, but she's going to get to the point where she misses him."

I lifted an armful of colorful mod clothes. Under the clothes were three clear plastic raincoats, white boots, and a pile of handbags. Scattered across the bottom of the trunk were scarves, pins, and costume jewelry. I set each item in a neat pile on the floor.

"Why do you think Ronnie wanted this stuff?"

"I don't know, but I don't think it had anything to with visual merchandising."

I yawned. As tired as I was, I didn't want to abandon my one chance to inspect the trunk. Something about it didn't add up. From the outside, it looked like it held more than I unpacked, but the interior had been full. There wasn't enough room for the contents to have shifted.

One of the scarves caught on something. I stood up and used both hands to remove the loose items, leaving behind a sheer ivory scarf that matched the trunk lining. It stuck to the seam. With a little effort, I released the scarf. I wound it around my hand like a boxer taping his knuckles, and I stared inside. A small, almost undetectable ivory tack jutted up from the bottom.

I grabbed a gold chain from the pile of costume jewelry and threaded it under the ivory tack, then gently pulled up. I encountered mild resistance, and then the bottom of the trunk popped out and revealed a secret compartment.

Under the false bottom, nestled next to a tightly packed pile of men's clothes, was a stack of sheet music and two reels of tape marked "Modifiers Album #2 – Master."

I smoothed out the sheet music. They were standard pages, ledger lines in sets of five, marked off on the left side with a treble clef. One by one, I turned the pages over. It appeared as if someone had been working out a song. I'd been so caught up in the likelihood that Boyd was a spy that I forgot all about him being a musician, especially one who walked away from his career at its peak.

If I had any remaining doubts about why anyone would spend fifty thousand dollars on a sealed trunk, this finding erased them. Sixty year old clothes barely held their value to collectors but recording masters of an unknown second album along with accompanying sheet music could be worth a lot — to a whole different crowd.

19

ONCE A MOD, ALWAYS A MOD

"This trunk originally belonged to Beatriz Jones," I said. I pointed to the wall that faced the street that faced the Kirkville Hotel. "I met with her earlier tonight. Across the street. She said the trunk was hers and she left it with Boyd when they broke up." I picked up one of the reels of tape. "She never mentioned that there was a second album."

"If he hid it in the false bottom of her trunk, she probably didn't know it was there."

The music memorabilia brought up an entirely different motive for obtaining the trunk. Boyd died without a will, and his unclaimed estate defaulted to the crown. That meant there were no heirs. Who would stand to profit if this album were found and released? What was the life of a recording contract from the sixties?

"How'd you find this Beatriz woman? I thought this

trunk was the property of an unknown person. Unknown implies unknown."

"Her number was on Ronnie Holiday's phone. She called the newspaper about the trunk too. I was following leads, and when I called her, I asked to meet face to face. I didn't know of the Boyd Brighton connection until we talked. And Ronnie was holding a Boyd Brighton album when he died."

"I thought he was holding his phone," Eddie said.

"He had his phone in one hand and the album in the other."

"No wonder he drove into a tree."

I dropped the false bottom back into the trunk and leaned back. "I keep telling myself Ronnie was a just a sixties enthusiast who wanted some mod memorabilia. He looked like an extra from *Quadrophenia*."

"Once a mod, always a mod."

"Not according to Beatriz. She said mod was just a phase."

"You know the connection between fashion and politics. Being a mod is more than how you dress. It's a belief system. Looking forward. Challenging norms and expectations. Seeing the world through the lens of possibility, not nostalgia and routine. You don't change out of it when your clothes are dirty."

Eddie was right. There were a lot of people who dressed unconsciously, putting on some version of what they wore the day before, but when you looked back at photos from different eras, there was always a dominant style of the time. It was only in recent years, when designers simply mined the past for current collections, that style became more novelty than political commentary.

I narrowed my eyes. I'd spent a lot of time with Eddie since moving back to Ribbon several years ago, and if anybody asked, I'd say I knew him well. But something about the way he said that sounded dismissive. As if he knew something I didn't.

"Are you a mod?"

"Sure."

"Shouldn't you self-identify so other people know?"

"Other mods know."

"*I* didn't know."

"I always assumed you were a rocker. You wear a black leather motorcycle jacket and you have a thing for bad boys."

"Nick's not a bad boy."

"He has ties to the local mafia."

"Point taken."

History, as I'd learned it, was defined by hemlines and shoulder widths. It fascinated me to learn that during World War II, there had been government directives on fashion that kept collar shapes, skirt lengths, and other minor details from changing so women wouldn't feel the need to shop to stay au courant. Almost every notable change in fashion history had been a symptom of the times, from jeans in the late eighteen hundreds to miniskirts in the sixties. And because I studied fashion history as my major in college, clothing became an unspoken language that I used to assess the people I encountered. I leveraged my college degree into a career at Bentley's New York department store and learned that the business of fashion attracts all kinds. Once you're surrounded by people who are compensated with samples sales and discounts, you realize an interest in fashion does not an interest in history make.

Sometimes a cigarette pant is just a cigarette pant.

"I'm not a rocker," I said. "I like motorcycle jackets because they're classic and they remind me of *Grease 2*. I like pinstriped pantsuits because they remind me of *The Godfather*, and I like sequins because they remind me of Cher."

"Don't sweat it. If your wardrobe represented your belief system, you'd dress like Columbo."

I relaxed against a fixture and scanned the rest of the trunk's contents. White socks, tasseled Weejuns, a tweed overcoat, a poor boy cap, and a slew of scarves. A color-blocked sweater and a narrow, four-button suit. Eddie reached in and pulled out a Navy blue Fila zip-front jacket. "Righteous."

"Keep it," I said. "I haven't seen a dime of money from Ronnie Holiday so technically, this stuff is still mine. Consider it partial payment."

Eddie didn't argue. He slipped on the jacket and zipped it over his T-shirt. "Every once in a while it pays to be your friend. Go home and get some sleep. I'll take care of the merchandising so you can impress your new boss."

I picked up the recording masters and sheet music.

They had to be central to the mystery. I reluctantly held out the store keys to Eddie. "Would you feel better if I promised you my salary?"

"That's an empty promise considering June July won't pass a background check. Your one chance at survival here is to blow Franny's mind before she finds out who you are, and for that you need an expert."

Eddie was right about one thing: Exhaustion had drained me and I craved sleep. I took the music memorabilia out of the trunk, replaced the clothes, shoes, and jewelry, and relocked the thing. I left Patti's car parked next to Eddie's VW bug and drove home in Loncar's Supra. I parked in my garage, double checked the door locks, and went inside. Logan was asleep on Nick's pillow. I tried to call Nick from the home phone but his call went to voicemail. I tossed my clothes in a pile on the floor, and crawled into bed, not bothering to shower off the day.

———

THE NEXT MORNING, I OVERSLEPT.

It took me a moment to remember why I was alone in the bed. Nick was a day into his Italy trip, and that's all the time it took for me to get embroiled in a new mystery. I wished he were here so I could talk over everything that had happened since buying the trunk, but we'd made a pact. If everything worked out, this trip could change the trajectory of his business. In the past, I'd shown support by trying to solve all of his problems (and creating new ones in the process). Now, support was letting him solve them himself.

I buried my face in his pillow and inhaled, then rolled over and tapped the phone on the nightstand to see what time it was. The phone screen was cracked. Last night flooded back to me: having Loncar in my pocket via a phone call, having the biker take my phone and throw it on the floor. I got up and removed Ronnie's phone from my handbag. I'd forgotten to plug the darn thing in and the battery was dead.

So much for the fish video.

I plugged in Ronnie's phone, showered, and dressed in a red and white horizontally stripped boatneck T-shirt, black wide legged trousers, and white running shoes with red and black stripes throughout the midsole.

The house in which I now lived was the house of my childhood. When my parents announced they were moving to the West Coast, I gave up my career in New York, moved back to Pennsylvania, and bought the place. The price was right and the owners didn't worry all that much about disclosure and emptying the attic before the new buyer moved in. I'd made a few changes in that time, mostly of a decorative sort. The answering machine was not one of them.

I fed Logan and cleaned out his litter box. (Dogs have owners and cats have staff, right?) I made a fresh pot of coffee. I recorded a new outgoing message on the outdated machine: *I'm unavailable. Leave your name and number at the beep*.

It was shortly after eleven. I was eager to tell Loncar

about what I'd found in the trunk when I dropped off his keys, so I chugged two cups of café au lait (coffee with enough milk to make it a chuggable temperature), ate a handful of pretzels, unplugged Ronnie's phone, and headed to Senior's apartment complex with the tapes and music in my bag.

I arrived at Nick Senior's apartment with my discovery in my handbag. I went into the lobby and waited for the elevator. The bell went sounded, and when the doors opened, Petra stood there. Today the restaurant owner wore all black covered by a green plaid apron. Her gray pixie was flat on both sides and spiky on top.

"Hi, Samantha," she said.

"Petra, hi. Are you feeling better?" She looked confused. "I talked to Phil last night and he said you were ill yesterday."

"I'm fine," she said hastily. "Phil worries too much." She stepped out of the elevator and kept her hand on the sensor so the doors didn't close. "Back to check on Senior's place?"

"I forgot to water his Ficus tree yesterday."

"He's more popular now than when he's here. When I travel, I hand my bamboo plant over to a friend, lock the doors, and don't think twice about the apartment until I get back. I'm starting to wonder if his painting of 'Dogs Playing Poker' is an original William Wegman."

The doors to the lobby opened, and Detective Loncar walked into the lobby. At seeing me, his face registered surprise. He held a cardboard cup holder with two large coffees nestled in it. He seemed to weigh his options—elevator with me, landing with Petra, stairwell in the corner of the building, or turn around and leave. He chose the path of least resistance and came into the building.

Petra looked a little confused at seeing Loncar. She excused herself and left us alone in the hallway. I glanced at the coffees and then at him. "That was considerate," I said. "I've already had two cups but I can always drink a third."

"Did I know you were coming here?"

"No. But I brought your—" I glanced over each shoulder and lowered my voice — "car. I don't know how much you remember about last night—"

The elevator doors opened and Loncar pushed me inside. I stumbled forward and put my hands out to regain my balance. The doors closed. "What was that about?"

"You shouldn't have come," he said.

"Why not? People in this building have seen me come and go from Senior's apartment since he moved in. There's nothing suspicious about me being here." It was at that point I realized Loncar had never once bought coffee for me. He didn't even offer me a cup from the pot in the corner of his office. And Nick's dad had a perfectly acceptable Nespresso machine in the kitchen and every type of coffee pod you could wish for thanks to my generosity at Christmas. There was another reason Loncar was acting cagey, and I wanted to know what it was.

We reached the floor to Nick Senior's apartment. "Wait out here," he said.

"No." I pulled out my keys and Loncar snatched them from my hand.

"Ms. Kidd, I'm asking for a favor. Stay out here or go downstairs and wait for me in the lobby."

I might have honored his request, but we'll never know. Because before I had a chance to walk away, the door to Nick's dad's apartment opened from the inside and Patti greeted us in Loncar's faded chambray shirt and little else.

THE COOLEST OF THE BUNCH

"Hey, Sam," Patti said. She took the coffee tray from Loncar and turned back inside. "I didn't know you were coming over."

"Neither did I," Loncar said under his breath.

I was speechless. Not because I didn't want the best for Loncar, but because just yesterday, he'd lamented the age difference between him and the lady coroner, and it seems all it took was a couple of drinks and the convenience of Nick Senior's apartment. The oddest part of it all was that when Senior found out, he'd be thrilled for the part his empty residence had played in the hookup.

Patti was the coolest of the bunch of us. She carried the tray of coffee to the kitchen, removed both cups from the carrier, and peeled off her lid. Steam rose from the surface. She bent over the cup, closed her eyes, and inhaled, and I swear, it was more seductive than the interrogation scene in *Basic Instinct*. I'd been drinking coffee my whole adult life and I'd never once considered the process sexy. Maybe I should take notes.

"Are you staying?" Patti asked. Before I had a chance to answer, she set her cup on the counter and pushed herself away. "Give me a sec. I'll be right back." She walked into the bedroom but didn't close the door. I didn't know women this comfortable in their skin, and I certainly didn't expect the ones that were to be in Loncar's league. Maybe he had game.

The casual way Patti treated her presence had the secondary effect of putting Loncar at ease. He stood a little straighter and cleared his throat. "Aren't you here for a reason?" he asked.

"Oh. Yes. Right." I pulled Loncar's keys out of my handbag. Loncar took them, tossed them on the counter, and then held the door open. I put my hand on the door and pushed it shut. "I know you want me to leave, but we need to talk about last night."

Loncar's eyes shifted away from me to the direction of the bedroom and then back to me.

"I don't mean *that*. I mean what happened at the Kirkville Hotel. While you were polishing off a flight of whiskey, I was chasing a lead, fending off an attack, getting you out of there safely, and discovering a new clue."

"I'm on the edge of my seat."

I turned away from Loncar and grabbed the extra coffee cup from the kitchen counter. I pulled the plastic lid off and held the cup out to him. "You're cranky. Drink some coffee."

"I gave up caffeine six months ago."

"Then why did you get two cups?"

"I asked him to," Patti said, returning from the bedroom. She'd pulled on her outfit from last night. Traces of black eyeliner smudged her eyes more expertly than in a Bobbi Brown ad. She carried an empty coffee cup in one hand and tossed it into the trash bin, then took the second one from me. "It takes me at least three to get going." She pulled out a bar stool and sat, drank more coffee, and watched us. "Are you guys talking about Ronnie Holiday?"

I stared at Patti, and then shifted my attention to Loncar. Patti had—or was soon going to have—vital information and her job required her to report it to the city, not to me. This was unfamiliar territory. But it was also an opportunity, and I could spare a few minutes.

"I'm in over my head," I said to them. "You know the woman I went to meet at the Kirkville Hotel?" I asked Loncar. He nodded. "Her name was Beatriz Jones. She told me the trunk was hers. She said she used to date Boyd Brighton and when they broke up, she left the trunk behind. I thought we were having a perfectly calm conversation until I said something about Ronnie, and she hinted that the regulars at the bar took care of him." I shrugged a shoulder, trying to impress Patti. "Considering what happened to Ronnie, I responded as if it were a threat."

"What did you say?"

"I may have implied that she was a suspect in Ronnie's murder."

"We still don't know that Mr. Holiday was murdered," Loncar said.

I looked at Patti. "Yesterday was a fourteen-hour day," she said. "I'm going to finish the autopsy when I get to the office, but that's the beauty of my job. Nobody's in a rush to leave."

"Well, if it wasn't a murder, then I don't think they would have gotten you drunk while they sent a guard dog to scare me."

"I wasn't drunk."

There were things I could have said: he passed out in my car, he snored when he slept, and he weighed far too much to depend on a person my size to support him but saying any of them would have ruined the moment. "I stand corrected," I said. "Still, a guy came to the back room where Beatriz and I were talking, broke yours and my phones, and told me to mind my business."

Loncar reached down to his pockets and patted them. "How'd he get my phone?"

"I'm no fancy licensed PI, but I think he plied you with liquor and then took it when you weren't paying attention."

Patti sipped her second cup of coffee. "You two should take this show on the road."

He-of-remarkable-focus continued as if Patti hadn't interrupted. "Did you?" Loncar asked. "Mind your business?"

"It depends on what you consider my business."

"Where did you go after Ms. Detweiler drove me home?"

"You still call her 'Ms. Detweiler'?"

Patti smiled at Loncar. "I like it," she said. "Has an air of dominatrix."

Loncar turned beet red.

"I drove Patti's car to The Mod Holiday to swap out with yours," I said to Loncar. I moved my hand back and forth between Patti and me. "That's what we thought was best."

"When you got to the store, did you drive straight home?"

"No. The lights were on at The Pho so I went there first and visited with the owner. Then Eddie Adams—you remember him, right?" I asked Loncar, who nodded — "arrived to do some visual work on my behalf, so when he pulled into The Mod Holiday parking lot, I left The Pho and joined him. While we were there, I unlocked the trunk." I flipped the top of my handbag open and pulled out the sheet music. "I found these inside. I don't know if Ronnie hid them or if they were there all along."

Loncar took the sheet music. He thumbed through them and checked the back of each one, then set the stack of paper on the table.

"Beatriz told me she's the owner of the trunk. She didn't say anything about a possible second album or new songs." I pulled the reels of tape out of my handbag. "These were in there too. If Boyd wanted to disappear, he wouldn't want the attention a second album might bring them."

Loncar picked up the tapes. "If these are actual recording masters, they might be valuable to a collector."

"How valuable?"

He shrugged. "It depends. The Modifiers weren't the Beatles, but somebody with the right connections might be able to drum up some interest. Could be there's something else on here and the label was intended to throw people off. I'll take them to my tech guy and find out."

"Who's your tech guy?"

"Geek squad."

"Fine, don't tell me."

I was beginning to see that, unlike me, Loncar didn't just drive around town randomly confronting people who may or may not have had something to do with a deceased person who may or may not be a murder victim. He had access to a network of professionals who could get answers a lot easier than a former fashion buyer turned amateur sleuth.

We bandied about theories for the next half an hour or so, nothing worth starting a murder board for, especially since we were in Senior's apartment and the nosy nelly property owner might frown at that sort of thing.

"What's your day look like?" Patti asked me.

"Everything's pretty fluid. My boss at the store expects me to merchandise the place, and my boss at the paper probably wouldn't mind a check-in, but other than that, I'm flexible. If you want to get your car, I can take you to it now."

But before we agreed on my proposed plan, there was a knock on the door.

21

QUITE A FAMILY

THIS WAS WHAT PEOPLE LIKED TO CALL A compromising situation. Senior was out of town, and three of us—none of whom were on the lease—were inside. I'd forgotten all about the smoke detector inspection, but I was the likeliest candidate to have a reason for being there, so our plans changed on the fly.

I opened the door. "Hi," I said. Two women waited outside the door: a fifty-something woman with dyed blond hair and overplucked eyebrows and Petra. The contrast between the two woman was comical: one trying not to look her age and the other looking younger because she didn't care.

"Samantha," Petra said, "I didn't know you were still here. This is Cathy, the property manager."

The woman with Petra spoke. "I'm here to conduct the smoke detector inspection."

"Oh, right. Senior said something about that. Come on in." I held the door open. She entered. I mouthed, "thanks," to Petra, who nodded. She turned away, and I closed the door. "I'm Nick Senior's daughter-in-law. He's out of town, and I'm house-sitting." I turned back to Patti and Loncar. Patti had her backpack slung over one shoulder. "I'll touch base with you both later."

Loncar lifted the tapes and documents from the counter and tucked them under his elbow, then ushered Patti out the door.

Cathy was all eyes. Senior had referred to her as a nosy nelly, and I wondered if she'd ever been in here before. If she was trying to covertly check the place out, she failed miserably. I followed her eyes around the room to see what she saw, including two coffee cups and my sightline landed on the rumpled bed. Oh no!

"Would you excuse me for a moment?" I asked. I went to the bedroom, stripped the sheets, and tossed them in the corner. Other than the bed, the room looked like Senior left it. I left and found the property manager in the dining room.

"So you're the daughter-in-law," Cathy asked. She pressed the button on the middle of the first smoke detector and a shrill beep pierced my ears. I shuddered from the unexpected loudness of it."

"Yes."

She left the dining room and went to the bedroom. If she noticed I stripped the sheets, she didn't comment. Instead, she said, "Quite a family you married into."

"Sure. Nick's dad is great."

She raised her eyebrows. "I've had three complaints about his poker games and one accusation that he dropped a water balloon onto a neighbor's car from his balcony. He harasses the maintenance staff with requests that don't go through the central office, and he refuses to pay the prorated customer charge of his rent." She pressed the button on the second smoke detector. This time I was ready for the sound and held my hands over my ears.

"What's the prorated customer charge for?"

"Everybody pays it." She moved on to the kitchen.

"That's not what I asked." I'd file the look she gave me under "hostile." "Has he asked what it's for?"

"There are expenses to maintaining an apartment complex."

"And they are?"

She pressed the button on the third smoke detector. It shrieked. "No other tenants have a problem with their rent statement, but Senior contests it every month. What does that say about him?"

"He's suspicious of a company that may be blindly ripping him off?" I offered as one possible answer.

Apparently "hostile" had layers. Like an onion.

The property owner made a notation on her clipboard and then walked to the door. "When's Senior due back?" she asked calmly.

"A few days."

She wrote something down. "If he has anyone staying here for over a week without notifying the front office, he's in violation of his lease agreement. Since the sheets were a mess when I got here, I'll assume you slept over. If your father-in-law isn't back in five days, he's evicted."

"Don't bother," I said. "When his lease is up, he's moving in with us."

I was almost sure Nick would back me up.

The smoke detector inspection kept me at Senior's place until after one. I was closer to the *Ribbon Eagle* than to The Mod Holiday, and I wanted to use the paper's resources to do some digging into Beatriz and Boyd Brighton, plus, with the broken phone situation, until I got a replacement, I needed a way to make calls.

The bullpen was quiet. Yesterday's staff meeting had left everyone with assignments and deadlines, and Monty must have laid down the law because the air of festivity that went with the anniversary party was absent.

I stopped by Kristi's cubicle on the way to mine. Her light blond hair was expertly secured to the top of her head in what appeared to be a hair donut. She wore a loose cotton floral sundress over a white T-shirt. Her giant sneakers were blue. She scrolled through a slew of images on her computer screen.

"Hi, Kristi," I said. "Remember the other day when I unlocked the trunk from the auction? Didn't you take pictures for the blog?"

"Yes," She said. "I already told Carl I deleted them."

"Why would Carl ask you about my unboxing pics?"

"Didn't Monty tell you? He gave the story to Carl."

That made no sense. "There must be a mix-up. Let me find out what's going on."

I left Kristi's office Carl was standing in his cubicle. He kicked the base of his chair.

"Problem?" I asked sweetly.

"I can't get the height adjusted. Every day I get it perfect but the next day it's off." He bent his head down and fiddled with the seat adjuster. I snickered. He straightened back up. "You."

"Me?" I asked innocently. "What could I possibly have done to your chair?" It was too much trouble to suppress my laughter, so I gave in.

"I'll get you back," he said. He held out his hand. Now hand them over."

"Hand what over?"

"Your notes. Everything you have about Ronnie Holiday. You're back on fashion." Monty wants you to give me whatever you have since I'm playing catch-up."

There was no way I was giving Carl my story! Not after everything I found last night. "Do your own legwork. Or better yet, beat me to the story."

"That's cute, Kidd. You might have a knack for sniffing out mysteries, but you're still an amateur. Stay in your lane."

"I'm in my lane, and my tank is full. I have no intention of pulling over and letting you pass me."

I expected Carl to either run with the driving metaphor or return an equally juvenile comeback, but he picked up his phone and pressed one. "She's here," he said, "and I don't think she knows."

A moment later, Monty's office door opened. "Kidd!" Monty bellowed. "My office. Now."

I didn't have a good feeling about this. Monty may have pulled me into his confidence from time to time, but Carl *was* the paper. I left Carl looking smug and went to Monty.

"Close the door."

I pulled the door shut. Monty leaned back in his leather desk chair and it creaked under his weight. "The story goes to Carl."

"Why?"

Monty gently rocked back and forth, and his chair squeaked in protest. His tie was askew. He studied me for a moment, and then answered. "I got a call from the coroner's office this morning. Do you know how Ronnie Holiday died?"

"He drove into a tree after overdosing on cocaine," I said.

"He OD'd, but the coroner found evidence that the overdose wasn't voluntary. Earlier this morning Ronnie Holiday's death was ruled a homicide."

22

NOT MY STORY ANYMORE

I WASN'T SURPRISED. ALL ALONG, I'D SUSPECTED FOUL play. The thing keeping me from knowing for sure was a full case load at the coroner's office.

"Who did you talk to?" I asked.

"The coroner's assistant," Monty said. He straightened his crooked tie. "I confirmed it with the police. Anything you've learned about Mr. Holiday should go to Carl."

"I've spent more of my time talking to people who were interested in the trunk. That's my story, remember? I can follow up with them."

"That's all background to a crime story."

"What about the weekend supplement and prime web placement? What about my six inches?"

"I gave them to Carl too."

"Then what's my assignment?"

"I don't care. Pick a local retailer and do a profile. Four hundred words." He pointed at his door. "Now get out of my office and get back to work."

I went back to my cubicle with steam coming out of my ears. The first thing I did was call Patti. I was under no illusion that she'd call me first with information related to a murder investigation, but I was curious about the information Monty shared.

"Coroner's office," she answered.

"Patti, it's Samantha."

"I've been expecting your call," she said. "I don't have a lot of time. The police are here."

"Then it's true? Ronnie Holiday's death was a homicide?"

"Yes. There was a small puncture mark at the base of his skull. It showed up in the film I left with my lab tech last night. He confirmed it with a tissue sample and a second round of tests and reported it to the police this morning before I got here."

"You said Ronnie died from a lethal dose of cocaine. Does the puncture mark fit that scenario?"

"Yes. It's not a common spot for an injection, which made it easy to overlook. I can't picture how it played out, though. His stomach and digestive tract were empty so he didn't ingest it through food. If someone approached him from behind, they'd have to be swift. Otherwise it would take two people: one to restrain him and another to deliver the drug."

I closed my eyes and recalled the night Ronnie died. I'd watched him pull into the parking lot of the Kirkville Hotel, circle around the back, and then drive from the exit into oncoming traffic and crash into a tree in The Pho parking lot. "What if he were in his car? What if he was talking to someone through his window?"

"It would have been easiest if his seatbelt was on, but it wasn't."

"Unless it was."

A picture emerged. Ronnie lowering his window to talk to someone behind the hotel. That someone injecting him with cocaine. Him trying to free himself—unhooking his seatbelt—and then driving away? "Wouldn't the cocaine have made him super-alert?"

"I don't know how much detail you want, but the overdose caused Mr. Holiday to have a stroke. Driving into a tree was what broke his forward trajectory, but he was dead before the accident. If you want to stop by later, I can give you an interview for your story."

"It's not my story anymore."

"Why not? I called you right after I filed my official report. Your intern said he'd give you the message. I thought that's why you called."

"What intern?" I stood up and looked over the tops of the cubicles. Kristi and Oswald were by the coffee. Carl raised his hat and bowed, and then sat back down.

"Carl something," Patti said. "He thanked me for the phone call and said he'd make sure you got the message."

Oh, I got the message, all right. "Thanks. I'll talk to you later."

There was a story there, and it was mine. It started with the trunk. Since then I'd found a cache of passports and a cufflink that could have been made by Q. I infiltrated The Mod Holiday, the coroner's office, and the Kirkville Hotel where I talked with a suspect and got threatened by a thug. I'd discovered unreleased tapes from a pop-star-turned-spy.

I admit, it sounded a little unbelievable.

I've never scooped Carl on a story. We worked together once, and he knew he never would have gotten the story he did if it weren't for me, so that time we shared a byline. This time was different.

I was done playing second fiddle. This was my best sleuthing to date, and I wasn't going to just hand it over to Carl because my boss said so.

Actually, that was a pretty sound reason for doing so, but I had one thing going for me: Carl's entire story relied on what I knew.

I called Carl's extension. "Don't you have a message for me?"

"Here's a message: the story's mine," Carl said. "I'm waiting on your notes."

There was another thing going for me: the need to return fire on the practical joke front. If I could pull this off, it wouldn't just be a professional coup. Carl had it coming.

I opened a notepad and wrote *Ronnie Holiday Murder?* at the top. Underneath, I added notes: *Born in a town called Malice. Suffered from Quadrophenia. Collected Eton rifles and butterflies.* I added several Post-Its for good measure: *Leads: David Watts? Irish Jack? Uncle Ernie? Skaface? Paul Weller in the library with the lead pipe?*

I shoved the notepad in a folder and closed it, and

then grabbed my bag and headed to the exit. "The notes are on my desk, Collins," I called out. "Good luck with the story." I got onto the elevator and called Kristi from the garage.

"Do you want to help me play a joke on Carl?"

"Sure!" she said.

"Remember those photos you took after José cut the lock off the trunk?" I asked.

"I told you, I deleted them. You said we weren't supposed to have gotten into the trunk."

"You didn't delete them. You think you deleted them. Go to your photo app, go to albums, and scroll down to recently deleted. Send me everything, and don't tell Carl. And Kristi?"

"Yes?"

"Delete them when you're done."

I hung up. The way I saw it, my folder of fake notes was like a tipped bookcase that gave me a marginal cushion of lead time over Carl. But he wasn't inept. It was largely due to his profile on me after I exposed a local mobster's influence in our town that my life changed. From there I received that massive windfall I mentioned, but with fame comes the absence of anonymity. Carl took away the one thing that allowed me to run around town asking questions without being known. Now the only way for me to succeed was to become a secret agent myself.

23

DESPERATE FOR CLIENTS

I DROVE TO A PHONE STORE AND TRADED IN MY broken phone for an upgraded replacement, had them swap out my SIM card, and left. A backlog of text messages from Nick came in on my way out the door.

Flight delayed.

Landed. Tired.

Busy day. Can't call until late tonight.

Something unexpected came up. Tonight's out. Sorry. Love you, XO.

I typed back a brief response: *Broke my phone. Got a new one. Love you too. XO.* I considered adding an emoji but couldn't decide between the pretzel and the eggplant. I added a heart and hit send.

For a trip that required eight hours of air travel plus hours to and from an airport, Nick didn't have a lot of downtime. We'd discussed this back when he first set up the meeting with Blak and agreed the last thing he should worry about was making time to call me. If this trip were to work, Nick would need all of his attention focused on the photo shoot during Blak's free time.

I installed the Burner app and set up April May, and then added a third number for June July. I drove through McDonalds and ordered everything I thought would be good for a hangover then drove to Loncar Investigations. We had unfinished business, and I assumed I'd get more face to face than over the phone.

Loncar's Supra sat behind the building, so I parked out front. The reception desk was vacant, and the door to Loncar's office was open. He stood over the printer as it chugged out papers. I knocked on the doorframe to announce my presence. I wasn't sure what sort of welcome to expect (it could go either way), but he nodded his greeting and then nodded at the chair across from his desk. I set the McDonalds bags on his desk and removed an order of fries for myself.

"Do you remember Carl Collins?" I asked.

"Sure."

"Patti told him the results of Ronnie Holiday's autopsy. Now he knows it wasn't an accident. My editor pulled me from the story, but I'm doing it anyway."

Loncar picked up the paper from the printer tray and set the set the stack in a file folder. He peeked into the McDonald's bag and pulled out a Big Mac container. We sat in silence for a few minutes while we ate.

Loncar finished his Big Mac and dumped his trash into the paper takeout bag. "Patti wasn't Carl's source," he said.

"She was, but not intentionally. She thought she was

leaving the information for me." I ate three more fries and then pushed them away. "Did you already call them?" I glanced at the door behind me. "Are they on their way?"

"Who?"

"The police. I was at the restaurant when Ronnie drove into the tree. I should tell them what I know."

Loncar drummed his fingers on the outside of his file folder. "Let them come to you."

This was new. I leaned forward and propped my elbows on the edge of his desk. "We're not going to cooperate?"

"They're conducting an investigation. They have a system. Your name is on record as being at the restaurant. If they want to talk to you, they know where to find you."

"But—"

"Let them do their job."

I pulled Ronnie's phone out of my pocket. "—won't they want this?"

Loncar stared at the phone. "Did you tamper with it? Delete files? Erase the call log?"

"I played a fish video on repeat and called Patti to help me get you to Senior's apartment."

Loncar held out his hand. Reluctantly, I handed the phone to Loncar. He dropped it into a yellowy-brown paper envelope and sealed it, then wrote "R. Holiday phone" on the outside and dropped it into a desk drawer.

"I'll get it to them."

There is, perhaps, no better distraction than new evidence, which Loncar used to his favor. He handed the manila file folder to me. I opened it and scanned the documents while he took his seat behind the desk. Inside were copies of newspaper clippings, printouts from websites, and a summarized bio of Beatriz Jones.

"What's this?"

"Background. Part of the job."

"Oh. Yes. Right." He took me seriously? After I tried to pay him with pink money? Either I was growing on him, or he was desperate for clients.

"Beatriz Jones worked as a receptionist for the record label that signed the band. She dated Boyd for two years, one and a half of which they spent living together. They broke up around the same time the band broke up, and several strongly-opinioned voices in anonymous chat rooms believe the breakup was the catalyst for the band dissolution."

"What a cliché."

Loncar continued. "She moved to Southern California, where she peddled juices at a natural food restaurant, then eventually migrated east. I documented jobs at four diners and one ice cream stand. She eventually landed in Philadelphia around the Bicentennial and started work as a perfume spritzer at Wanamaker's, where she remained until she turned sixty-five. She retired and moved to Ribbon."

"If I didn't know you, I'd think you spent your spare time studying fiction. Have you found out anything about Boyd? Why he had a bunch of passports and a James Bond cufflink?"

"I haven't figured that out just yet."

"Good. Now you have an excuse to keep racking up billable hours."

Loncar raised his eyebrows. "If I didn't know you, I'd think you were planning on stiffing me for my work."

"You'll get your money, I promise." I closed the folder. "Now, let's get down to business." Loncar's eyes shifted from me to the folder and back to me. "Personal business. What happened last night?"

"According to you, my memory of last night is not reliable."

"I'm talking about you and Patti."

"I slept on the sofa."

"Yeah, right. Patti obviously slept over. How'd it happen? What did you say?" I put my elbows on his desk and rested my chin on them. "I'm an old married woman now. Tell me everything."

"Speaking of which, when is your husband due back?"

The day after tomorrow."

"Does he know about any of this?"

"He was with me when Ronnie died, but he left the next day. He already had a full schedule planned before his dad decided to go with him. We agreed his focus should be there, so I told him not to worry about me until he gets back."

Loncar seemed impressed. "You're okay with that?"

"I trust Nick completely. Besides, the record shows

I'm much more likely to get into trouble than he is. Now back to my question. Do you like her?" I asked.

"I'm not going to discuss my love life."

"So this was more than a drunken hook-up? Because if it wasn't, then you wouldn't care. And you probably wouldn't have complicated your professional life by getting involved with someone you'd rely on when you need autopsy results."

"Did your boss assign you a different story when he pulled the one you've been working on?"

Of course Loncar would try to distract me by bringing up the case now. "Monty wants the story. He doesn't care which one of us gets it. Carl's been playing practical jokes on me since I started using the April May byline. The best way for me to get him back is to beat him to the scoop."

"How do you plan to do that?"

"After I work off my debt to Eddie, I'm going back to the auction house. A lot of people have come out of the woodwork to get a trunk that cost me fifty bucks. I'm going to sniff around and see what I can find."

24

STUCK IN THE PAST

I SPENT THE AFTERNOON WITH EDDIE ON HIS citywide beautification project. The local vandals had returned to Borough Hall, this time expressing their dissatisfaction with local parking laws. I came home smelling like turpentine. The obscenities were gone and for the next five minutes, Eddie and I were even.

It was seven thirty at night. I changed into a black A-line dress, black and white checkered tights, my mom's black Bernardo booties, and headed out to the auction.

The Harrington Auction House was a nondescript building on the edge of Ribbon. It shared a parking lot with a café that closed by three p.m. which worked well for both business's conflicting hours. The only people to miss out were the auction attendees who craved a caffeine fix.

It was the final day of the Boyd Brighton auction. The parking lot was speckled with cars, a fraction of the crowd that had turned out for the opening. As I approached the front doors of the single-story building, a breeze kicked the hem of my dress, exposing more of my checkered tights than I would have liked. I kept my hands at my sides to hold down the fabric until I was safely inside away and from any more nature.

The room was filled with a mostly male crowd. Attire ranged from black leather to olive green parkas. As I scanned the room looking for familiar faces, the auction barker rallied the crowd to increase bidding on a 1961 Epiphone Wilshire solid body electric guitar. The bidding was at six thousand dollars and volleyed back and forth between a man in a Who T-shirt and a man in a black leather motorcycle jacket. The first man was a stranger, but the second was not; it was the man who tried to steal the trunk from the *Ribbon Eagle* offices. I didn't believe it to be a coincidence.

I made my way to the bar and ordered a club soda with lime. I peeled off a twenty dollar bill and dropped it into the tip jar. "Do you know anything about the man in the black leather jacket who keeps running up the bids?"

The bartender, a youngish guy with longish hair, reached into the tip jar and pulled out my twenty. I thought he was going to hand it back, but he folded it over and jammed it into his jeans pocket. "That's Vince Rodriguez," he said. "He's a regular at the auctions. He used to teach music at the local high school but there was a scandal and they fired him."

"You don't know anything about the scandal?"

"Who's asking?"

"Samantha Kidd," I said. "I'm doing an article for the paper."

The bartender shrugged. "I heard he used a weighted scale to grade the kids who bought equipment from his store. Some parents found out and complained and the school board ditched him."

I turned my shoulder to the youngish bartender and sipped my club soda. "What does he do now?"

"Still runs a music shop. Teaches private lessons. Hasn't been here for a while but sure seems interested in this auction."

"What makes you say that?"

The bartender picked up a glass and buffed it dry with a linen tea towel. He cocked his head and looked at his tip jar again. I was starting to understand Loncar's day rate. I peeled off another twenty and dropped it into the glass.

"He's been here every night this week."

A woman in a red and white shift dress and a man in a black blazer got behind me in line. I held out my cup for a refill of club soda, and the bartender topped me off. I stepped out of the way and scanned the rest of the room. I'd paid almost as much for my information as I had for the trunk. I was either a sucker, or I was getting the hang of sleuthing. I didn't know which.

I scanned the crowd and kept my eyes on Vince. Auction lot after auction lot, he outbid his competition. Did private lessons pay that well? Or did Vince have a line on a secondary income source that connected back to the trunk?

The next lot was a set of 1967 Sunn amplifiers. The program said Boyd Brighton had given up his musical career in 1964, so these were either miscellaneous musical equipment that got bundled into his auction, or they indicated that, despite Boyd's professional retirement from music, he continued to play for his own pleasure. I hadn't thought much about him and his choice to hang up his rock star shoes (Clarks desert boots or Bass loafers, if he stuck to his mod aesthetic), but that was the reason this whole auction had drawn interest. Boyd Brighton was, at one time, poised to be the next Pete Townsend, but something had happened to make him throw it all away.

But he hadn't. He'd kept it. The estate of Boyd Brighton indicated that for all of Boyd's forward thinking and modern posturing, he was stuck in the past. Something about that was hinky, but I couldn't work out what.

I finished my club soda and then sat in the back row of the auditorium and made notes. We got through a couple of home-built guitars that looked like a high school shop project, a Vox AC-15 amplifier with cabinet corners, and a natural blond Model 325 Rickenbacker with a Kauffman vibrato. All three went for double the estimate in the catalog thanks to Vince and his ability escalate bids.

I turned my back on the auction and walked toward the payment window. A gaunt man worked the counter. He wore a NASA T-shirt and cargo pants.

"Hi," I said. "I was here on opening night. I bought the trunk of an unknown woman."

The man tapped a placard that was positioned next to the register. "All sales are final." He made a face that might have been a smile.

"I'm not interested in a return. I'm doing an article for the newspaper and thought it might make a nice angle to talk to people who were interested in the trunk and find out why. Explore the auction mindset."

"If I gave you that information, the auction could not be called 'silent,' could it?" He made his is-that-a-smile face again.

"I see your point." I drummed my fingers on the wooden counter and looked around the interior. The auction was over. I turned the other direction and watched a stream of people leave. I returned my attention to the man behind the counter. "Can I leave contact information with you? Maybe the auction house can notify the interested parties on my behalf?"

He set down his pen. "Listen. I already told your editor that information is confidential."

"You didn't talk to my editor."

"You're April May, right?" The man slid open a drawer and pulled out Monty's card. "Is this your editor?" He held the card and looked at me. I nodded. A numb sensation radiated outward from my chest. Monty didn't follow up on cases or track down leads. He didn't undermine his reporters. But he'd been the one to assign this story to me. He had an unnatural interest in the trunk, and I'd never found out why.

The man dropped the card back into the drawer. "You can leave your information, but I can't promise anything." He pulled a notepad out of a drawer and slid it toward me.

"Sure, okay. I guess you have to be extra careful ever since the data breach."

"Funny you mention that," he said. "The exposed information was from the silent portion of the auction, and that's the least profitable aspect. As far as computer glitches go, it could have been worse."

It must be nice to go through life not suspecting anyone of anything. I envied his residency on Planet Normal.

I jotted down April's phone number and hastily scribbled her name, then added "Trunk of an Unknown Female," underneath. I thanked the man. I turned back to the auction and scanned the room for Vince, but he was nowhere to be found. I left the building and found him waiting for me in the parking lot.

25

SHAME, INNIT

I WASN'T PREPARED FOR A PERSON—ANY PERSON—TO be standing directly outside the exit, and I was prepared even less for it to be the man who tried to steal the trunk.

Vince stepped back from me and held his hands up in the air, the tip of a lit cigarette marking a small orange dot against the dark sky. His black denim jacket was covered in band patches. His black jeans were skinny and shredded. One black belt, studded with silver, was in the beltloops of his jeans and a second belt of similar style was worn loose over the top of them. His shoes were chunky black leather boots with silver metal reinforced at the toes.

"Whoa, mate, he said. "In a bit of a hurry, are ya?"

"I didn't realize how late it was."

"Early's more like it. The night's just getting started, innit?"

My hand closed around the can of pepper spray

Loncar gave me. There were plenty of people around, but if Vince tried anything, I could protect myself.

Now that I'd recovered from our near crash, I recognized the opportunity to get something for my troubles. I didn't know how best to approach the subject, so I went with a cross between shock value and gossip.

"Did you know about Ronnie Holiday too?" I asked. Vince drew a long inhale from his cigarette and then exhaled, breathing a steady stream of smoke over the top of my head. He didn't move his eyes off me.

"Who's Ronnie Holiday?" He stretched Ronnie's name out, emphasizing both the "Ro" and "die" and dropping the "H" in "Holiday."

I pointed across the street. "The man who bought the trunk you tried to steal from me at the newspaper office." Vince didn't seem to care that I remembered where I'd seen him. "He died a few days ago," I added.

I tried to pay attention to his body language, but the cloak of darkness, combined with the cloak of black denim and leather, conspired to make observations impossible.

"Oi," Vince said. He took another pull on his cigarette. "How'd he die?"

Something kept me from telling him what I'd learned. "Car accident," I said. "He ran into a tree."

Vince exhaled again and then tossed his cigarette to the ground and stamped it out. "Shame, innit."

He started to leave and instinctively, I knew I needed

to keep him there. I'd gotten nothing from him so far, and April May was better than that.

I said the first thing that came to my mind. "Can I bum a cigarette? I'm fresh out."

"Sure," Vince said. He pulled a pack from an inside jacket pocket and shook one loose. All I had to do was light it and channel Barbara Stanwyck. I put it between my lips, and Vince held out a lighter. I sucked on the end and then fought the urge to cough, spit, or throw up. Undercover work was no joke.

"You knew him, didn't you?" I asked.

"We've met."

"It's a funny thing, that trunk. Ronnie wanted it too. Why all the interest?"

"I can't speak for my mate, but I'm a collector." Vince said. His eyes moved from my face to my hand. I had one arm wrapped around my waist and my other elbow propped on my hand with the cigarette between my fingers like I'd seen a women do on film a hundred times. "You going to smoke or not?" he asked.

I looked at the tip of the cigarette glowing bright against the darkness outside. It had burned down about a quarter with no help from me. I felt lightheaded and dizzy from the first inhale and I wanted nothing more than to rinse the taste from my mouth with Listerine.

"This isn't my regular brand." I tossed the cigarette to the ground and stubbed it out with the toe of my (mom's) bootie. "Besides, I've been meaning to quit."

Vince leaned down close to my face. My hand

tightened around the pepper spray and I tried to pop the cap off with my thumb. "You didn't see what you think you saw," he said. His breath smelled like nicotine. "Now leave me alone." He stormed past me and went back inside.

Right before the door closed behind him, I called out, "Don't you want to know what I found in the trunk?"

I wasn't sure if he heard me, and I wasn't sure if I wanted him to. I stood there, outside the auction house, with the faint scent of smoke and tar fading in the air around me, wondering whether I should cut my losses and leave.

I wanted to leave.

But I couldn't. Not without knowing why Vince responded so aggressively to me. I opened the door and poked my head into the auction house. Vince was at the payment counter talking to the gaunt man in the NASA T-shirt. The employee handed something to Vince. Even from a distance of twenty feet, I recognized it as the same notepad on which I'd written my name and number. I released the door and backed away from the entrance, then retreated to my car.

It was one thing to insert myself into a situation. It was quite another to know I was the one being inquired about. Despite a cache of fake names, I felt overly conspicuous.

I drove home on autopilot, my mind distracted by questions. I knew the answers were just beyond my reach, but even with three identities to choose from, I was quickly becoming known in all the wrong places.

THE NEXT MORNING, I WOKE TO SOMETHING TICKLING my arm. I opened one eye and saw Logan swatting at my arm with his little black paw. As soon as my eye was open, he tipped his head and butted my hand.

"How come you don't do this when Nick's here?"

He meowed.

I got up and tended to his majesty's food and litterbox needs, then showered and dressed in a white Lacoste shirt, red cropped, wide-legged corduroy pants, and black penny loafers. I pulled on a black Baracuta G9 jacket and left.

The trunk brought me into this mess, and the trunk was supposed to be my jumping off point for a story for the paper. When Monty pulled the story, he told me to fill my space with a story about a local retailer. He knew I had relationships with most of the boutiques in Ribbon; I covered their events, reported on their expansions, frequented them as a customer. I could call the owners of any number of stores and set up a photoshoot and an interview in an afternoon.

I'd been distracted by the trunk—the McGuffin we'd all spent too much time focused on—and not by the common thread: Ronnie. Everything started when he walked into the *Ribbon Eagle* offices. I'd learned a lot since that morning, but I still didn't know why Ronnie wanted to overpay for a trunk he could have bought for a tenth of a percent of what he offered me or why Monty told me to take the deal.

I closed my eyes. Ronnie and Monty. Monty and Ronnie. Monty was the one who greenlit my story about the trunk, and Monty didn't care about fashion. Monty was the one who called me away from the trunk to meet with Ronnie, and he was the one who told me to sell it. Monty had gone back to the auction house and asked the same questions I had—questions about who wanted the trunk.

I didn't know if Monty had seen inside the trunk when José cut the padlock off, but he was the one who assigned Kristi to photograph the unboxing. Monty gave me the padlock from his file cabinet to reseal the trunk. Monty gave me the combination.

Monty. Monty. Monty.

I had to find out what my boss's connection was to Ronnie Holiday, and as much as I hated to admit it, there was only one person I could count on to help me get at the truth.

———

FOR A WHOLE BUNCH OF REASONS, STARTING WITH MY suspicions of Monty and ending with my need for neutral ground, I made plans to meet up with Carl at Dough Re Mi. He was already at a table when I arrived. His straw hat sat on the table next to half eaten bagel smothered in cream cheese. I approached the table, and he pushed the plate aside. "I assume you're here to give me your notes?" he asked.

"I gave you my notes."

"David Watts?" He rolled his eyes. "Uncle Ernie?"

I smiled. "What you give is what you get." I dropped into the chair across from him. "Speaking of which, where's my money?"

"Is it technically your money? I thought you bought the trunk from petty cash."

"I took fifty dollars from petty cash. There's a lot more than fifty dollars in that envelope, or there should have been. Did Ronnie give you money? Or did you make that up too?"

"He gave me money. It's in Monty's safe."

I couldn't believe Monty was in on the joke. He didn't like when we used newspaper resources on gags, and he didn't exactly share his vault combination with the rest of us.

"I waited until he left the other night and put it in. He gave me the combination last year."

"But the safe is in his office, and he locks his office when he leaves."

"I made a copy of Monty's keys two years ago." Carl tried to hide his pride, but he did a poor job.

"Does he know?" I asked. Carl averted his eyes. The answer to asked and unasked questions were clear: Monty had no idea Carl had access to his office off hours, and now I knew how we would find out what Monty was hiding.

"We have a problem."

Carl pushed his chair away from the table and put his hat on his head. "I can do the story with or without your notes. It makes no difference. The police report is a public record. I already got quotes from the owner of the restaurant where the victim died and the coroner's office confirming the cause of death."

"Monty's involved in the murder." I let those two words hang in the air for a moment, and then, when Carl didn't call me Brenda Starr, Lois Lane, or Vicky Vale, I continued. "He's the one who told me the paper was in trouble. He told me to sell the trunk to Ronnie. He tracked the story the whole time and we both know he doesn't care about style stories. And after Ronnie died, Monty changed his mind about everything and turned my story into a showpiece that was going to get weekend exposure. He did a complete about face, and it feels like whatever it was he wanted to keep hidden was no longer a threat."

Carl sat back down. "You're sure about this?"

"It's no joke, Carl. Monty's somehow connected to Ronnie Holiday's murder."

"You're wasting your time."

My hope plummeted. After a month of practical jokes, no way was Carl going to trust me.

"Come with me to the paper. Monty has an appointment this morning and everybody else is working from home. If we're going to find out anything, it's going to have to be now."

26

SNACKS

CARL LEFT THE BAKERY, AND WE DROVE IN SEPARATE cars to the newspaper office. It was inefficient, but trust was thin on both sides of our tenuous partnership. He reached the newspaper office before me, but to his credit, he waited in a chair outside Monty's office.

"Don't get used to it, Kidd," Carl said. "I waited so you can't accuse me of keeping information from you."

"If Monty's lying about the paper, it affects us both."

"Monty isn't a murderer," Carl said.

I wanted to believe him, to have the same blind faith in our editor as he did, but I knew things Carl didn't, like how Monty had contacted the auction house. And even though Carl covered the crime beat, I'd seen firsthand how people could get pushed beyond their limits and commit crimes. Something was up with our editor; I just didn't know what.

"How do you want to do this?" I asked.

Carl pulled a set of keys out of his jacket pocket and unlocked the door.

Monty's office was neat. If delegating were an Olympic sport, Monty would have medaled. He kept confidential source information locked in one file cabinet and payroll information locked in another. A third cabinet, the one Monty removed the padlock from, was unlocked. I slid the top drawer open and looked inside. The interior was packed with boxes of Girl Scout cookies. "Snacks," I said. Carl peeked into the file cabinet and shook his head. I slid the drawer shut and opened the drawer below. It was full of Coke cans. At least now I understood Monty's immunity to the afternoon slump.

I slid the file cabinet closed. Carl sat in Monty's chair. He logged into the computer and searched the hard drive. I sat in the chair across from Monty's desk and flipped through his paper calendar.

I set the calendar down and went around the back of the desk so I could see Monty's screen. Carl accessed Monty's search history. About a month ago, there was a block of clicks on the auction website.

"When did you pitch the story to Monty?" Carl asked.

"I didn't. He assigned it to me." Carl turned away from the screen and looked at me.

"Didn't you think that was strange?"

"No. I write a style column. It seemed like a fit."

Carl shrugged. "Sometimes I envy how you fly under the radar."

"Right. Like you're jealous of me."

He turned to me. "You've got a long leash around here. You pitch a story, Monty greenlights it, and you're off and running. I've watched you email your column from home more than once."

"I have no budget, and when your stories go too long, mine are the first ones he cuts."

"He gave you an alter ego so you could author more articles for the paper. That means he wants to exploit your talents. Don't sell yourself short, Kidd. You may have been just a style columnist when you first came here, but now you're part of the team."

Carl leaned back and the chair made the same noise it made when Monty did the same thing. It made me wonder if Carl did it because he'd watched Monty do it a hundred times first, or if the chair was just that comfortable.

"Does Monty have a calendar on his computer?" I asked.

"Yes. Why?"

I pointed to the paper calendar. "Why would he keep a paper calendar and an email calendar? Isn't that overkill?"

"Maybe. Give me an appointment and I'll see if they match up."

I called out Monty's recent dental appointment. "Yep. It's here. Give me another." I called out the date of his car inspection. "That's here too."

"What about..." I ran my finger down the calendar

page. "March sixteenth. He circled the date and wrote 'payment.'"

Carl tapped a few keys. "Nope."

I flipped backward and found another circled date. "Same thing on February sixteenth."

Carl typed something. "Nope."

I sat back, defeated. Monty had a recurring appointment on his calendar that he didn't record online, and that hinted at something he didn't want others to know. But without more information, I was at a loss.

I sat up. "Check his credit card statement."

Carl glanced at me. "Sure. Tell me what bank he uses and I'll get right on that."

"I don't know! I'm grasping here. Look up the one our checks come from."

Carl typed again. "Give me login credentials and we're all set."

Another dead end. "I think better when I'm full. Do you want some cookies?" I asked.

"Cookies are just going to lead to a sugar crash."

I tipped my head back, dangled my arms on either side, and kicked my feet out in front of me. I was the picture of giving up.

I went to the file cabinet and pulled out two cans of soda and set one on the desk for Carl. I popped the top of the other one and drank as much as I could before the carbonation burned my throat. Even though the soda was room temperature, the sugary-sweet flavor hit the spot and instantly revived me. I kicked the file cabinet drawer closed and turned around.

Carl popped his soda and chugged half. He set his can down and burped. "It's almost worth being here to discover Monty's stash."

"You didn't know about the soda and cookies?"

"How could I? He usually keeps that file cabinet locked."

Carl was right. Monty took the padlock off the cabinet for me to use on the trunk. He must not have had a chance to replace it, but the bigger question was why did he keep soda and cookies locked up?

I dropped down to my knees and pulled the file cabinet drawer open again, this time lifting out the cookies and the Coke. The good thing about working with Carl was that he had a streak of curiosity that rivaled mine. He joined me. I didn't know what we were looking for, but I felt certain there was something hidden in here that didn't have a calorie count.

I dumped the soda cans onto the carpet and sorted them one by one. The second to last was empty. I shook it for good measure, then reached for the pull-top.

"Don't!" Carl exclaimed. He held both hands up in front of him to shield off a spray of sticky sweetness, but when I popped the top off, inside was a small bank ledger. It showed regular five-thousand-dollar withdrawals from the newspaper payroll on dates that corresponded with Monty's paper calendar.

"Do you know anybody who gets regular off-the-books payments?"

"Nope."

"Me neither." I sat down on the floor. "Monty's been paying someone off with newspaper resources." I flipped through the ledger and a business card fell out. It was the same as the one Ronnie Holiday gave me the day he showed up at the paper. On the back, under ~~London Paris Milan~~ *Ribbon* was a phone number. "Was Ronnie Holiday a source?"

"I never heard of Ronnie Holiday until you brought that trunk into our lives."

"Same here. But these payments go back six months." I chewed my bottom lip and thought.

"Why was Monty paying Ronnie five thousand dollar payments ever month?" I asked Carl.

"Because he was blackmailing me," Monty said from the doorway. "Ronnie Holiday was a bottom-feeding scumball. The world's better off without him."

27

GET OUT OF MY OFFICE

I COULDN'T SPEAK FOR CARL, BUT I'D BEEN SO immersed in the paper trail we accessed that I hadn't heard the elevator or the doors. One could argue whatever investigative prowess we'd demonstrated by finding the hidden documents was negated by being so out of touch with our surroundings.

Monty loomed in the doorway. I never noticed before how intimidating he was; one could call him a big guy. The bullpen behind him was dark, and the light behind him came from the hallway. I was familiar with his surly attitude, but today, it translated differently. Carl and I were alone in the offices with a man who had something to hide, and we were the two who stood between it being exposed or being kept secret. I didn't yet know Monty's secret, but with one dead person involved, it seemed prudent to proceed cautiously.

"Blackmail," I repeated. "What did Ronnie have on you?"

"You don't know?" Monty asked.

"I know you paid him money from the newspaper budget. I'm not making excuses for whatever he did, but that's embezzlement."

Carl remained silent. For an investigative reporter, he sure was letting me handle the heavy lifting.

"What do you know?" Monty demanded.

"Enough to see you tried to hide it."

Monty looked from me to Carl and back to me, then back to Carl. "Who wants to walk me through your research?"

I glanced at Carl. His face was cast in distorted shadows and light, making it difficult to read his expression. His silence spoke volumes. He turned to me and nodded.

"When you told me to sell the trunk to Ronnie, you gave me the padlock from the file cabinet behind your desk. When we looked in that file cabinet tonight, it was full of cookies and soda."

I suppose that didn't sound wildly suspicious, so when Monty didn't speak, I kept going. "It seemed strange for you to lock up cookies and soda, so we emptied out the drawer and found a can with a false bottom and a bank ledger that lined up with the dates on your paper calendar."

It was an impressive piece of investigation if I did say so myself, but Monty offered no praise. He crossed his arms. "Why are you here?"

"You lied," I continued. "About the paper being in trouble. You told me to sell the trunk to Ronnie Holiday because the paper needed the money, but we don't. Subscriptions are up, and Oswald has advertising booked and paid for until the holidays. We might be the only privately-owned paper in the country that has more money coming in than out. What I can't figure out is *why* you lied."

"Get out of my office."

I looked at Carl. He made no effort to move. My knees were a little sore from kneeling on the carpet, but I was staying put, solidarity and all.

"You owe us the truth, and before you say we can't handle it, you should remember we're the reason subscriptions are up. If anybody can spin this to make you look good, it's probably one of us."

Monty scowled. "I don't like it when Carl sits in my chair. He readjusts the settings and it takes me two days to get it back the way I like it. We'll talk in the conference room."

I stood and followed the two men to the conference room. The blinds were closed and the room was dark. Monty turned on the overheads and all of a sudden, it was time for a board meeting. Monty took the head of the table and Carl and I sat next to each other on the same side.

"I never wished I had lazy reporters until today," Monty said.

Carl pulled his phone out and turned on the recorder app. He set it in the middle of the table. Monty swatted the phone off the table, where it hit the cabinets then bounced onto the floor. "Off the record."

Carl picked up his phone, tapped the screen, and dropped the phone into his pocket. "What's your connection to Ronnie Holiday?" he asked.

"Which one of you put that together?" Monty countered.

Carl pointed at me and I pointed at him. We couldn't have planned it better if we'd tried.

"Figures you two would work together on this." Monty sighed. "A couple years ago, a friend of mine approached me about buying into an investment deal. It was for a bundle of properties around Ribbon that had a high turnover rate. They were cheap because tenants rarely stayed in business. As a bundle, they had a chance of turning a profit in five years. Rents for the occupied properties would cover the shortfall for any vacant properties over time, and as the infrastructure of Ribbon got stronger, tenants would stick around. Less turnover meant more profit."

"So you formed an LLC and bought the properties," I said.

"We formed a shared trust."

"What's the difference?"

"Ownership remains in the trust when any one grantor dies. There's no transfer necessary so we avoid probate."

"Who's 'we'?"

"Doesn't matter. My partners are both deceased." Carl and I exchanged glances and Monty cleared his throat. "We're not spring chickens at our age. When you eat pork three meals a day, you don't stack the odds in your favor."

It seemed too convenient, Monty buying into a shared trust then having his partners die off. "Let me guess. When they died, their shares conveniently defaulted to you."

"Do you want to hear this or do you want to make up your own narrative?" Monty turned to Carl. "Collins, tell her what I told you when you came to work here."

Carl faced me. "Don't try to bully the truth out of a cooperating source. Treat him like a friend of the paper. If the story checks out, that's what he is."

"Fair enough," I said. "So?"

"The guy who put the deal together, his shares defaulted to his wife. When she sorted through his paperwork, she found out he didn't have the money he told her he did. The properties were vacant, and vacant properties don't make money for their investors. Her husband was the grantor of the trust. When I bought her out, the trust transferred to me. That's when I learned the paper was one of the properties in the portfolio."

"Wait a minute. You own the *Ribbon Eagle?*"

"By accident, but yes."

"How did you not know?"

"We bought into a bundle of properties as silent investors. The deal was to put up money and then sit back and cash checks. The value of the portfolio was in the bundling of properties, not in any one of them. A property manager handles the lease agreements." He waited a beat and then repeated, "Silent. Investors."

Carl pressed Monty on the details and a fuller picture emerged: when Monty bought out the wife of one investor, he obtained the details of the investments. The *Ribbon Eagle* offices, the very spot where we sat, was among them. And Monty was now part owner, officially conflicting his interest in the news.

There were obvious questions circling the conversation: why Monty never sold and what this would mean to the employees. In the shorter term, calling what Monty had done with the payroll "embezzlement" was a little murky, since the profits he appeared to be skimming were already his. And while Carl hounded Monty about his lapse in judgment, I couldn't help bringing it all back to the murder.

I put my hand out to silence Carl. "What does any of this have to do with Ronnie Holiday?"

Monty leaned back. He crossed his arms and stared at Carl. Carl stared at me. I didn't need Monty to answer to know the connection. "You also own Ronnie Holiday's store," I guessed. "He found out your secret and that's why you wanted me to sell the trunk to him."

"Holiday was one of my tenants," Monty said. "I don't know how he found out which properties I owned, but he did. He's been blackmailing me for the past six months. He approached me a month ago and offered me a deal: if I obtained the trunk from the Boyd Brighton auction for him, he'd leave town and I'd never hear from him again."

Which explained why he assigned the trunk story to me, but not why Ronnie wanted the trunk in the first place.

"And you trusted him? You thought he'd leave you alone?"

"Hard to say. When people like him get their claws in you, it takes something big to make them let go. We'll never know now."

I glanced at Carl, wondering if he was thinking the same thing as me. Maybe Ronnie would have gone away, but maybe not. Technically, Monty's problem with Ronnie ended the moment Ronnie died.

28

WELL PLAYED, KIDD

THE LONGER CARL AND I QUESTIONED MONTY, THE less suspicious I was about his motivations. Not only did I have experience working for him, but his story rang true. There was no reason for him to tell us what he had unless it was the truth. He knew Carl would keep on digging to see there was a news story there, and me? I'm just curious that way.

"You told me to sell him the trunk because you knew it would get him off your back, but after he died, you wanted me to run with the trunk story. Why?"

"I'm a newsman to my core, Kidd. Holiday paid more for that trunk than he extorted from me." He drummed his fat fingertips on the table surface and leaned back. "Would have been a good story if I knew why he wanted it."

It was easy to see Monty's conflict. This was a man who'd built a career on digging out news stories and reporting them, maybe not on a grand scale, but in his own way, to his own audience. The *Ribbon Eagle* wasn't a huge operation, but it wasn't a joke, either. For a small town, we had an interesting mix of wealthy folks and criminals, though the two were certainly not mutually exclusive. I lucked into my position here, starting out as the subject of a feature, then contributing a guest column, and now a staff writer, but Carl and Frank, our sports guy, had worked here for decades. They were proud of what they put out every day.

And Monty had built that. I didn't want to believe he'd throw it all away over a murky situation like this, but I had one more question to ask. "Where were you the night Ronnie Holiday died?"

Monty drummed his fingertips on the table again. He stood up, and I thought he was going to storm out of the office. He pulled his wallet out of his back pants pocket and removed two slips of paper. "I took my wife to dinner in Lancaster. Stayed for dessert and the meter ran out. I got a parking ticket." He tossed two pieces of paper on the table. "Receipt and ticket are both time-stamped."

I reached forward and picked up the ticket. My theory about going end to end of Ribbon in twenty minutes didn't matter. Lancaster was southwest of Ribbon. The Kirkville Hotel was southeast. There was no way Monty could have done both.

I was happy to discover Monty wasn't a murderer, but I was back to square one. I turned to Carl after we left the conference room. "Take the story about Ronnie," I said. "I'm going to write about Boyd

Brighton. I went back to the auction last night and I think I have enough for a puff piece."

"I'll give you what I have on his background."

I doubted Carl's background on Boyd was as thorough as Loncar's, but it was a nice gesture. I followed him to his desk and called José from his phone. "Hi, José," I said so Carl knew who I'd called, "Can you bring the original legs to Carl's desk back to the newsroom?"

Carl's eyes widened. "You messed with the legs on my desk?"

José laughed. "Joke's over? I never got to see his face." I hung up the phone.

"Well played, Kidd. Well played."

I left the newspaper office and drove to The Mod Holiday. I didn't know how long I'd be able to keep showing up to "work," but I wanted back into the trunk. Franny still thought I was June July, her new employee in charge of visual merchandising. I had a cover story and a lead—and surely, Monty wouldn't want that to go to waste.

I called Eddie on the way, but he didn't answer. I left a message telling him to call me if there was anything I needed to know before I arrived. By the time I pulled into the parking lot, he hadn't returned my call.

I wasn't sure what to expect, but Eddie and his visual talents did not disappoint. The exterior of the store had a giant bullseye in blue, white, and red, visible from a mile away. The interior barely resembled the warehouse-feel of yesterday. On the far wall, he'd filled in the

Mondrian-inspired mural: intersecting bold black lines against a white background, with random blue, red, and yellow squares filled in. Fixtures had been repositioned throughout the store to allow for easier movement between them, and clothes hung by color, not by style. Racks of red, white, blue, yellow, and black sat intermittently throughout the shopping area. Round rugs, also in shades of red, white, and blue, sat in front of floor length mirrors installed throughout the shop.

Another wall was solid white with two arrows, one pointing up and another pointing down. In the back, where Franny had stacked boxes of shoe inventory, Eddie painted the wall in black and white checkerboard, then used clear plexiglass shelves to display black and white Chelsea boots against their opposite color background. I already knew Eddie had mad skills when it came to merchandising, but how he'd done so much in so short a time was beyond me. I was mostly impressed that the place didn't smell like paint.

"June!" Franny called out. She held a bunch of Pan Am reproduction flight bags in her hand. "You must have been here all night."

"I—right. I was."

"You'd never know it to look at you. I need your skincare routine."

"Cold cream," I said. "And once a week, I steam my face over freshly cooked pasta."

"Fine, don't tell me," she said. She set the Pan Am bags on the counter and joined me in front of the Mondrian mural. "I am impressed. Once you clean up the paint smears on the back door, this place will be fabulous."

"What paint sm—" I stopped talking abruptly. If I had done this, then I'd know what paint smears she meant. "I mean, it was so dark when I left last night I didn't realize I smeared anything."

"I figured. It wouldn't be a big deal, but it's the red paint, and that makes it look a little gruesome. Can you deal with that first?"

"Sure." I hastened toward the exit. Eddie wouldn't have left paint smears. He was a professional who didn't make those mistakes, and he had a trunk full of paint remover thanks the graffiti problem. Eddie would have told me if there was anything I needed to know before walking into the store today. Regardless of who was getting credit for the job, he would have done it right.

I went through the hallway and pushed open the back door. On the outside, a red handprint wrapped around the door as if someone had been holding it: palm print on the outside, fingers on the inside. Franny was right; it was out of place compared to the rest of the studied concept. But what she didn't realize was that after I cleaned the paint from the door, everything would be far from okay.

Because resting on the gravel outside the door was a black and white checkered Vans sneaker. And I knew beyond the shadow of a doubt that Eddie hadn't been sloppy with the paint. And Eddie hadn't missed my call.

Eddie hadn't called me to tell me what to expect because Eddie was in trouble.

29

DEFINE "OKAY"

EDDIE WASN'T THE ONLY PERSON IN THE WORLD TO wear black and white checkered Vans. Rationally, I knew that. I was drawing a conclusion based on half of a pair of shoes that were possible the company's number one selling style.

But I knew Eddie. I knew him. And that sneaker was a sign. It made sense. If Eddie's apartment went up in flames and he could only grab one thing, he'd grab those sneakers. Come to think of it, Eddie had an unnatural attachment to black and white checkered Vans.

I turned in a circle and scanned the parking lot. I'd been known to imagine a thing or two and sometimes made crazy claims. But this one felt...scary. I'd been here last night. I swapped out Patti's car for Loncar's. What if someone had been watching me? What if someone knew the trunk was inside? And if they saw me go inside after I left the Kirkville Hotel? What if someone saw me leave and confronted Eddie after I left?

I put my hand on the door to stabilize myself and touched something sticky. I pulled my hand away and my palm was red. The paint on the door was still fresh.

My universe felt as if someone tightened it with a socket wrench. My chest was tight, my legs were rubbery, and my imagination went wild. My memory flashed on the cause of Ronnie's death: lethal dose of cocaine injected by force, and the thought of losing my best friend almost rendered me immobile. My fear was followed with heat, boiling, motivational heat that knocked away the distractions of my external world and zeroed in on how I could help.

I wiped the smeared paint on the edge of the door and pulled out my phone and called Eddie again. This time I left a message. "Dude. Call me back. It's urgent."

As I stood in the parking lot outside of The Mod Holiday, trying to piece together what had happened and what it meant, my phone rang. It was Eddie. I swiped to unlock it and answered.

"Hey," I waited a brief moment and then said, "Are you okay?" No reply. "I'm at the store and you're not here. Where are you?" I pressed the phone against my head and plugged my finger into my other ear so I could hear his response.

"Dude," he said. "You could have warned me."

Relief flooded my every extremity. "You're okay?"

"Define 'okay.'"

"Where are you? Warned you — what happened?"

"I'm at home. I finished decorating the place a little after three. I propped the doors open to get some air inside and crashed on a pile of parkas. I woke up to some big guy lifting me off the ground."

"Who was he?"

"How should I know? I was half asleep and more than a little high on paint fumes. I took a swing at him, and he swung back. The next thing I remember is waking up in the parking lot with a black eye and one shoe."

"I have your shoe."

"Good. I was going to call you later, but you've been blowing up my phone. You owe me."

"I always owe you."

A breeze blew past me. It snaked inside the collar of my jacket and left my exposed skin covered in gooseflesh. I turned my back on the breeze and shielded my eyes as I stared at the roll-off trash bin now overflowing with empty boxes, packing peanuts, and paint cans. "Are you sure you'll be okay?"

"I'm chilling with an ice pack and a documentary on maple syrup. I'll survive."

As soon as the call disconnected, I ran to my car and cranked up the heat even though it was seventy degrees. I locked the doors and called Loncar and willed him to answer, and those three rings felt like five hours.

"What now?" Loncar asked.

"Someone assaulted Eddie," I said, not bothering with hello, how are you, or shut up and listen. "He was at the store overnight. He said a big guy came in looking for something. He woke up Eddie, Eddie took a swing at him, and the guy punched him back. The next thing Eddie remembers is waking up in the parking lot."

"He doesn't know what the guy wanted?"

"It's obvious, isn't it? Eddie was at the store. The guy wanted the trunk."

"Where are you calling from?"

"The store."

"Hold tight, Ms. Kidd. I'll be there as soon as I can."

"One more thing. My boss here thinks my name is June July. Eddie is my brother, August. You can't show up asking questions as a private investigator or Franny will be suspicious." I looked up. Franny had exited the building and was scanning the parking lot. Whether she was looking for me or Eddie or evidence to an assault she may or may not have played a hand in, I didn't know. If I wanted to know what happened last night, then I had to act like nothing was wrong. I turned off my car and got out and waved to her so she knew where I was. I pointed to my phone to indicate to her that I was busy, and then turned my back on her and lowered my voice. "I have an idea," I said.

"What's that?"

"Come to the store and follow my lead." I bit my lip and then continued. "Your code name is Dad." I hung up before he could protest.

I put Eddie's shoe in my car and then went back inside. I couldn't discount Franny as a possible player in Ronnie's murder, and for that reason, when I returned to the interior of the store, my guard was up. She could have had a hand in Eddie's assault. Until Loncar arrived, I trusted nobody.

Franny was behind the counter stuffing the Pan Am flight bags with wads of tissue paper. "What time did you leave last night?" she asked.

"I didn't look at the clock. Why?"

"Because I'm paying you hourly, for starters." She didn't seem pleased. "If the place didn't look so good, I might think you're being vague so you can pad your timesheet. As it is, I don't know how you did it." She shifted four bags to a pile by her feet and then lined up four more and started stuffing them one by one. "How'd you get in? I don't remember giving you keys."

"Ronnie provided a set." Was that a lie? Not technically. "I left them at home."

"I'm going to need that set back. I wish you would have told me that first."

"Sure." I approached the counter and picked up a sheet of tissue paper to help her.

She knocked my hand away. "I've got this. As long as you're here, you can fill out your hiring paperwork. I left it on the desk."

"Okay." I glanced over Franny's shoulder to where Eddie and I had buried the trunk. It was gone. I swept my eyes across the rest of the floor behind the register, left to right, but it wasn't there.

"Do you need something else?" Franny asked.

"Where'd the trunk go?" I asked before thinking twice. I pointed over Franny's shoulder to the spot where it had been. "The one your uncle bought at the auction."

She glanced up and then back at the tissue paper. "Why?"

I narrowed my eyes and assessed her. She'd indicated hostility toward her Uncle Ronnie from the first day I walked in here, and now she was being cagy. Aside from the work Eddie had completed last night, I didn't know what had transpired here or if she was a part of it. All I knew was that she wasn't off the hook.

"You said it was the least of your concerns," I said. "I mentioned the trunk to my dad, and he's interested in buying it. He's on his way here now."

"Why would your dad want a sealed trunk? You don't even know what's inside." She rested her hands on either side of the Pan Am bags. "Or did Uncle Ronnie provide a key for that too?"

If I'd been unsure about her tone earlier, there was no mistaking it now. Franny might like the merchandising, but she didn't like me.

I answered the way I thought a person not embroiled in a murder investigation might. "He collects them. Old trunks from different eras. That one looked interesting. His birthday is coming up, and I already told August about it. I thought if Dad liked it, we could buy it for him and it would be one less thing for you to worry about."

"That trunk was the last thing my uncle ever contributed to this store. Did you think about that?

That I might want to keep it for myself as a connection to him?"

"I thought you and your uncle weren't close."

"You ask a lot of questions."

It was the same thing Vince had said. Asking questions was making me look suspicions. If I were going to keep it up, I needed a better cover, but I was running out of months.

I turned around and surveyed the interior. There was no denying how great it looked. Either Franny never intended to keep me on the payroll, or something else was going on. Something that made her want to get rid of me and keep the trunk—the very same trunk she wanted nothing to do with yesterday—to herself. But I couldn't leave. I couldn't lose access to the store, not now.

I left Franny out front and went to the office to fill out my paperwork, but when I reached the office, an entirely different set of papers that caught my attention.

Apparently Ronnie had a hand in more than one pie. On the desk was a legal brief and several canceled checks. Ronnie had been suing the restaurant next door.

30

SOMETHING WAS MISSING

RONNIE WAS SUING THE PHO? FOR WHAT? AND WHY hadn't Petra said anything?

It was then I remembered her awkward conversation the day she dropped off the Vietnamese honeycomb cake. She said she was worried I'd find out that she and Ronnie had a fight, but this was far worse than a disagreement. This indicated financial ruin. Petra had been at the restaurant the night Ronnie died. And since then, she'd popped up unexpectedly. Twice. And her husband said she hadn't been feeling well.

Murder, I imagine, can have a negative impact on your appetite.

I didn't know how long it would take Loncar to show up or what he was going to say when he did. I also didn't know how long Franny would leave me unattended in the office, especially now that she had questions about how I'd gotten Uncle Ronnie's keys.

There's a belief that when faced with a problem, you can either charge ahead and try to solve it, or let the solution present itself. Lacking the options for trying to solve this particular problem myself, I lowered myself into Franny's chair and started on my paperwork. At least if I was in the office with the checks and the legal brief, they weren't being handed off to someone else.

In my pocket, my phone buzzed. I pulled it out and read a text from Loncar: *close*. The man didn't mince words. I texted back: *OK*.

I now had more problems than I could count. Franny thought Loncar was on his way to make an offer on the trunk, but what we wanted had nothing to do with the trunk. But if Franny were guilty, then leaving suddenly, abandoning my pursuit of the trunk, would let her know I no longer needed it — which might tip her off that I already had what she wanted.

Maintaining my cover, maintaining my plan of distraction, maintaining my cool while Eddie was recovering from an assault, it was adding up and adding up and adding up and I was barely able to keep up with the sum of it all. I wasn't built to be a spy. I didn't compartmentalize things like they do in the movies. For the first time in a long time, I saw that my biggest limitation was my ability to care for other people, and I wouldn't give that up for anything.

Of course, that didn't help me now!

I filled out the employment papers with my fake name, my burner number, the address to my favorite pizza shop, and debated what to write on the social security number line. A car pulled into the lot. I peeked out the small window. Two blue Supras were parked side by side. I watched Loncar stand by the car and look over the building, then walk toward the back door. I abandoned the paperwork and greeted him with the checks and legal brief in my hand. "Look at these."

Loncar scanned the documents first. "Did Petra mention this to you?"

"No. She's been acting strange though. This is probably why."

He folded the papers and slipped them inside his jacket. I held out the canceled checks and he waved them off. "What did you tell your boss about me?"

"I told her it's your birthday, and I called you about the trunk. She thinks I'm up to no good, so you need to sell it. I'll tell you everything when we leave."

"You're April?"

"I'm June! Eddie's August." I had a sudden, scary thought. "Is this too much for you?"

Loncar glared at me. "Get back inside, and act naturally." He gave that a moment. "Unless that's too much for you?"

I glared back at him and then returned to the office. I scribbled a series of numbers into the social security number field in a messy enough scrawl that it would be difficult to read, and then neatened the pile of papers and went out front. The entrance door chimed and Loncar walked in the door.

Franny looked up and called out a hello. I quickly

followed it with, "Hi, Dad." Franny looked at me, and then back at Loncar, and I was a little offended that she seemed to be gauging the family resemblance. I turned to her and said, "I look more like my mom."

Franny turned back to Loncar. "June says it's your birthday."

"That's right."

"Are you named after a month too?"

"May," he said, and then blinked a few times. "Mayfield." He held out his hand for her to shake. Why was he wasting time on formalities?

Franny seemed as surprised by his outstretched hand as I was, but she dropped the shirt she folded and grasped his hand. "Franny Holiday. I've never met a family of people named after months before. Is it a family tradition?"

His face softened. "It was my mom's idea. We had a big family. She named us after the month in which we were born so no one would forget a birthday."

Sheesh! Between Eddie and Detective Loncar, the July family was due to get their own series! "My wife and I kept the tradition with August and June." When he said June, he glanced at me.

"Dad, Franny doesn't want to sell the trunk. It's got sentimental value for her. I'm sorry you made the trip out here for nothing."

Loncar's face returned to his normally gruff exterior. "Can I see it?" he asked Franny. "The trunk."

"I'm not sure that's necessary," I said at the same

time Franny said, "Sure." She went into the back room, and I grabbed Loncar's sleeve.

"We don't need the trunk anymore."

"Indulge me. It's my birthday."

Franny dragged the trunk into the store. Loncar didn't offer to help, which struck me as not particularly gentlemanly. Franny released the trunk by Loncar's feet. The padlock was gone. She undid the hatch, then flipped the trunk open. "My uncle died recently, and this was the last thing he showed any interest in. I'm still not sure what it was about it that captured his interest."

"Where'd he get it?"

"The Boyd Brighton auction."

"Wasn't there another buyer on record?" I asked. "I'm certain I heard somewhere that a reporter from the paper was interested."

Franny and Loncar both stared at me, but neither one acknowledged my comment aloud. Loncar turned to Franny. "You've gone through it?"

"Once, but I'd like to go through it again." She leveled her gaze at him. "Sentimental value, like your daughter said."

"Of course," he said. "Ms. Holiday, can you spare my daughter for the day? We rarely get to spend time together."

"Sure," she said. "June's employment isn't official yet anyway. She turned to me. "I'll call you when your background clears."

I went back to the office and slipped the canceled checks into my handbag. I was never going to hear from

Franny. Whatever job existed here wasn't for me. This was it. The last time I'd set foot in The Mod Holiday as an employee. If there were something here, something that connected back to Ronnie Holiday's murder, I'd either have to remember it or break in to find it.

31

UNSTOPPABLE

THEY SAY LOCATION IS EVERYTHING, AND TODAY THEY were right. Petra's restaurant was next door, making it easy to confront her.

"How do you want to play this?" I asked Loncar as we crossed the parking lot. "Good cop/bad cop?"

"Can you act naturally?"

"Like natural-curious or natural-concerned? I have a range."

"Just go inside and order something. See how Petra responds."

We went into The Pho. It was lunch time, but the restaurant was quiet. The trash bins were empty and showed no signs of the overflow you'd expect after a crowd. A teenager stood behind the counter reading *Icon* magazine.

"Hi," I said. "is Petra here?"

The teen shook his head. "She's at home packing."

Loncar and I exchanged a glance. "Is she going somewhere?" I asked. Loncar remained quiet.

"Her husband is taking her on a getaway. It was a surprise."

"What about the restaurant?"

He made a show of looking at the empty dining room behind us. "I think I can handle the crowd."

————

NEITHER LONCAR NOR I WAS WILLING TO BE WITHOUT a vehicle, so we drove to Senior's apartment in matching cars while taking turns on who was in the lead. Loncar parked in the visitor's space, and I pulled into Senior's reserved space in the garage. We met in the lobby and took the elevator to Petra and Phil's apartment.

"How should we play this?" I asked. Loncar knocked on the door. "Okay, I guess we're going to wing it."

Phil answered Loncar's knock. "Samantha. Charlie. This is a surprise. Come on in." He stood back. "Petra, we have visitors."

Petra came out from the bedroom. She held a bathing suit in one hand and a terrycloth beach coverup in the other. At seeing me with Loncar, fear filled her eyes. She dropped the coverup and turned away from us.

"You can't run away from this, Petra," I called out. "I know about the lawsuit."

"What lawsuit?" Phil asked me.

I stared at Petra. "Does he not know?" She shook her

head. "Do you want to tell him, or do you want me to do it?"

Phil turned to her. "What's Samantha talking about?"

Petra slowly turned back. She bent down and scooped up the terrycloth garment and wrung it in her hands. Her eyes brimmed with tears.

"Ronnie Holiday was suing The Pho," I said. "Petra's been paying him off in five thousand dollar payments to keep from initiating legal proceedings."

"That's not possible," Phil said. "We have a joint account. I would have noticed."

"She's right," Petra said quietly. She avoided looking at any one of us. "I didn't lose my engagement ring. I used it as collateral for a loan to pay him off."

Petra swiped spilled tears from her cheeks. She put her hand on the back of a dining room chair and leaned on it. The joints creaked under the pressure. "He said our colcannon noodle dish made him sick on three different occasions. He was going to report us to the health board." She looked at her husband. "We put our life savings into that restaurant. If he went public, we'd be ruined. You can't recover from claims like that, especially in a small town like Ribbon."

I'd never seen Phil get angry, but this news was worse than losing to Senior at a poker game or getting a late delivery of cabbage. His face turned red and he balled up his fists. "Our kitchen is so clean you could eat off the floors. No one's gotten sick."

"Wait a minute," I said. "When's the last time Ronnie ate at your restaurant?"

"The day he died," Petra said. Her voice shook. "I'm so sorry, Phil."

"Hey, hey, hey," he said. He put his arms around her and consoled her. "You didn't kill that man," he said.

"He's right," I said. "If Ronnie said your food made him sick, he was lying."

Phil turned around and Petra looked around his arm. "How can you be so sure?"

"The autopsy," I said. I looked at Loncar. "Ronnie was injected with a high dose of cocaine which caused him to have a stroke."

Petra's face fell. "That doesn't mean he wasn't sick."

Loncar added, "His stomach was empty. His whole digestive system was empty. Ronnie hadn't eaten anything all day."

Ronnie had led Petra to believe her food made him sick, but if only he'd eaten it, it might have saved his life. There was nothing in his system to help absorb the high dose of cocaine that had brought on his fatal stroke.

"Then he made it all up?" Petra asked.

"It seems that way."

I rarely got to deliver good news, and watching Petra and Phil hug out their concerns and relief tugged at my heartstrings. It made me miss Nick even more than I already did. I glanced at Loncar, who was busy checking his watch.

Having discovered the truth about Petra's odd behavior and the legal brief, I wished Petra and Phil a good time on their spontaneous vacation and followed Loncar out of their apartment. As the door closed behind me, Petra called out my name. I turned around and peeked back inside.

"With everything else going on, I almost forgot. You left your book in the lobby."

"What book?"

"The self-help book. *I'm OK – You're OK.* I saw it in Senior's apartment the day I dropped off the bread. You must have left it sitting out by the mailboxes."

After finding the passports and the spy gadgetry in the cigar box that first night, I hadn't thought much about the book, but it was the one thing I'd taken out of the trunk before handing it off to Ronnie. And what was it Ronnie had said on his message to me? *I know who you are. I know what you did. Where is it?*

At the time of his phone call, he had the trunk. He had access to the contents of the trunk. He was holding Boyd Brighton's album when he fell out of the car, and if he'd been motivated to find something inside the trunk, the false bottom wouldn't have fooled him. That meant he knew about the recording masters.

And still, he knew something was missing.

When I first found the passports and the James Bond cufflink, I assumed they were the trunk's great secret. They supported my suspicion that Boyd was a spy. But the book had been in there too. And even though I'd thumbed through it and found nothing unusual, knowing everything I knew, I had to check it again.

Was the book the key? Was that why someone had roughed up Eddie? Did they think the book was still in the trunk because they'd been in the trunk and the book wasn't there? It didn't matter if Franny kept the trunk. In fact, the trunk being at the store was the best possible red herring I could plant. Because nobody knew what I knew: that the book had been with me all along.

This might be the first case in history where a self-help book solved a mystery. Fine time for me to turn over a new leaf!

It took me a moment to remember where I'd left the book. At Senior's place? Yes.

"I didn't—"

"Thanks, Petra," Loncar said. "Have a good trip." He ushered me out of her apartment.

"The book!" I exclaimed. "I can't believe I forgot all about it. How did it get to the mailboxes?"

"I put it there."

"Why?"

Loncar shifted his eyes so we were no longer making eye contact. "I didn't want Patti to think it was mine."

"You're joking, right?"

Loncar sighed. "I'm dating a woman half my age, and I haven't dated since the seventies. You seem to get something out of self-help so I thought I'd give it a try."

"Me? I'm a mess! I'm currently going by three different names and two of them came from a calendar!"

"You've been a mess since I met you, yet somehow you now have a job, a house, a husband, and a cat."

"I had the cat *before* I met you."

Loncar shifted his weight and ignored my correction. "Despite being told — repeatedly — that you have no business solving crimes, you've managed to outsmart both police and criminals. I've given up trying to stop you."

"With all due respect, ever since you retired from the police force, you no longer have the authority to stop me." An alarming thought occurred to me. "You didn't retire because of me, did you?"

"Ms. July."

"Ms. July is your daughter." I waited a beat. "Call me Ms. May." Loncar cracked a smile. "Back to the book. You said you took it. Where?"

Loncar stared past me and pursed his lips. He tapped the arms of the chair in a steady beat while he recalled the events of that night, and I watched his expression soften, and then freeze. His eyes cut to me to check if I were watching him (I was) and then away.

"Patti ordered delivery. I was awake by then. I took the book with me to the lobby and left it on top of the mailboxes."

"That book came from the trunk." I followed Loncar to the lobby. He stared at a wall-mounted row of metal mailboxes. Each one had a keyhole. Along the top, piles of spam, grocery store circulars, and the occasional "Wrong Address" letter waited to be tossed into the recycle bin. Someone had left behind a coffee cup rimmed with orange lipstick.

There was no book.

Loncar pointed. "I left it there," he said. He pointed to the spot above Senior's mailbox. "I was going to get it after Patti left."

"But Patti didn't leave."

"No, she didn't." he said.

I thought back to the last time I'd been at Senior's, the same morning I'd found Patti there with Loncar. I'd walked right past this row of mailboxes and hadn't noticed anything. Would I have recognized the orange paperback if it had been there? I felt sure I would have. Not because I knew at the time that the book was important, but because I'd held that book in my hands, and we tend to notice what's familiar.

While we stood in front of the mailboxes, the elevator doors opened and Cathy, the property manager came out. Today she wore a T-shirt with cat butts on it. She glanced back and forth between us and then approached the wall of mailboxes. She picked up two abandoned soda cups and a stack of grocery store circulars and then looked at us.

"I—we—misplaced a book down here and we were hoping—"

"That orange paperback?" Cathy asked.

"Did you see it?" I asked eagerly.

"I didn't just see it, I took it." She shook her head. "People are always leaving things down here. Once a week I collect anything that isn't postmarked. Petra told me it was Senior's. I was going to drop it off with a can of Raid when he returned."

I felt my forehead scrunch in confusion. "Why did you buy him Raid?"

"He left a shopping list behind and it said, 'bug killer.' I saw it when I inspected the smoke detectors."

I wanted to laugh with relief. "So you have it? The book? It's in your office?"

"Not exactly."

Loncar and I looked at each other. Loncar asked, "Where is it?"

Cathy turned around and pressed the elevator button. "Follow me."

The three of us piled into the elevator and rode to Cathy's and Senior's floor. We went past Senior's door and followed Cathy to her unit and into her living room. The curtains were open and revealed the parking lot. Without thinking, I went to the window and looked out at the parking lot. Ant-sized people got into and out of Matchbox-sized cars. Normal people doing normal things on a normal day.

"Samantha?" Cathy prompted. I was about to turn around when I saw a car slow to a halt in the row behind Loncar's Supra. A woman got out and approached the back of the car. She held a baseball bat.

Moments later, she knocked out a taillight, got back into her car, and drove away.

32

THAT'S IMPRESSIVE

"Hey!" I hollered at the thick glass window. I slapped my palm on it a few times. "What are you doing?" But seeing as I was ten floors up and the woman was already back in her car, I was pretty sure she couldn't hear me.

Who could hear me? Loncar and Cathy. "What happened?" Cathy asked.

"A woman drove up to Detective Loncar's car and smashed out his taillight."

As you can imagine, Loncar had a wildly different response than Cathy. He moved to the window. "What woman?"

"She drove off in that bluish-gray sedan," I said. I pointed to the vehicle easing out of the parking space. It was too far to make out details like license plates and make and model, but—

"That's a 2012 BMW 3-series sedan in Liquid Blue Metallic," Loncar said. He pulled out his phone.

I tore my gaze from the window to Loncar. "You really are a good detective. That's impressive."

"No, that's my ex-wife." He punched in a bunch of numbers and turned his back on us, disappearing into the bedroom.

"Your friend is about to discover the repercussions of pursuing a woman half his age."

"I don't get it. His wife divorced him. She moved on first."

"And most rebound relationships don't last, and she's already programmed her mind to believe he's the reason she doesn't get what she wants."

"I thought all was fair in love and war?"

"Oh, Samantha," Cathy said, patting my hand. "If that were the case, the world would be a very different place."

A minute later, Loncar stormed out of the bedroom. "Has anyone vandalized your car recently?"

"No—yes! Two days ago someone broke into my trunk."

He held up his phone. "That was her. Send me the bill for repairs." He strode toward the door.

"What about the case?"

He stopped with his hand on the doorknob. "I'd like to get back into that trunk. What time does Franny leave her store?"

"Seven."

"Meet me there at eight." He left.

I moved to the window and watched as Loncar hopped into his car and drove off toward the long-gone liquid metallic blue BMW. I suspected he already knew how to find his wife. It was funny; I'd been running around town lying about my identity, my job, and my ownership of a certain trunk, and it turns out the mistaken identity that led to vandalism was nothing more than a shared taste in blue sportscars.

While I stared out the window and contemplated Loncar's love life, Cathy disappeared into the bedroom. She returned with a copy of *I'm OK – You're OK*. I say copy because the cover was shiny and the book was brand new.

"What's that?"

"The book you were looking for. Did you already forget?"

"That's not the book."

"Of course, it is." She thumbed through it and then closed it and extended it toward me. "It's a reissue, of course, but it's the same book. I imagine there have been a few updates along the years. It has over," she turned the cover toward her and read the endorsement, "fifteen million copies in print."

"But I need the other copy."

Cathy pushed her left sleeve up and exposed a chunky men's watch that dangled like a bracelet around her wrist. "I know you want to impress your father-in-law, but I don't think Senior will react that strongly to receiving a new copy."

"You don't understand. I need the one that was in his apartment."

Cathy looked embarrassed. "I'm afraid you can't have

that one," she said. "When I carried it up here, I set it on the counter and accidentally spilled coffee on it. I left it sitting on my windowsill to dry out, but I felt guilty about the damage so I went out and bought a new one for him. I'm certain he'll understand."

"*You* don't understand. I need the original."

"The book—the dog-eared one—came from a trunk I bought at auction. Everybody wants the trunk and nobody knows I took the book out."

"You do have an active imagination. I'm sorry to tell you there's nothing of interest in the book aside from a few insights on transactional analysis and a rudimentary explanation of the parent, adult, and child aspects of each of our personalities. It's Psychology 101."

"Where is it?"

Cathy went to her kitchen and opened the pantry. Inside were three wire bins stacked on top of each other, each one holding different recyclables. She pulled out the bottom bin and dug around old newspapers, then produced the book. "See for yourself." She held out the book and I took it.

The book smelled like coffee. The once-vibrant cover was now dingy and the pages, already curled and torn, clumped together in wet chunks. I tried to fan the pages but the absorbed liquid had acted as a form of glue, sealing many of them together. If there was something unique about this book, then it would probably remain a secret.

I sat down on a stool and set the book in front of me. Ownership of the mystery trunk had brought me nothing but trouble. I thought the damage to my car related back to Ronnie Holiday and the trunk, but that vandalism now seemed unrelated. The trunk was in Franny's hands at The Mod Holiday. I owned the only things removed from the trunk, and I could throw them into a furnace and walk away from this whole mod nightmare unscathed. We both knew I would not. I am ill-equipped to walk away from unfinished business. Call it a character flaw.

Out of curiosity, I picked up the book and opened to a page slightly past halfway. The page described a game people play referred to as "why don't you yes but," and the examples given described one person offering solutions to another person's problem, only to, repeatedly, be met with, "yes, but" along with a reason that solution wouldn't work.

As a recovering problem-solver, I assumed to see myself in the role of the advice-giver, but I didn't. I recognized myself in the Yes, But. When people gave me advice, I countered with why their advice wouldn't work. Almost every version of this conversation ended in frustration on both of our parts.

Maybe there was something to this book that had nothing to do with mods, rockers, or spies. Maybe it was just a handy way to understand human interactions. Maybe I'd keep the copy Cathy bought for myself.

I closed the paperback and curled it like a magazine, then released it and set it down. A few of the pages that had been stuck together came apart. Something was wedged inside. I picked it up again and pried a folded piece of paper from where it was stuck.

"What's this?" I mused aloud. I slid a fingernail between the edges and flattened it out. Shaky handwriting said "unnamed boy" on the name field, and the remaining details indicated he was born in Brighton, England in 1965.

"Did you find something?" Cathy asked.

"A birth certificate."

Someone had gone to greater lengths to hide evidence of a secret baby than to hide the fake identities, the spy gadgetry, or the music memorabilia.

Now we were getting somewhere.

33

VERY MUCH NOT OKAY

I FLIPPED TO THE COPYRIGHT PAGE AT THE FRONT. There was only one year printed on the copyright page: 1967. "This is an original copy. This birth certificate has been hidden in this book since the late sixties."

"This book doesn't belong to Nick's dad, does it?" Cathy asked.

I shook my head. "It came from Boyd Brighton's estate sale."

For everything Cathy provided regarding the contents of *I'm OK – You're OK*, she seemed completely in the dark with regard to Boyd. "Should I know who that is?"

"He was the lead singer of a mod British band in the early sixties. They had one record, and it was a commercial success. He became the face of the mods and that's all anyone wanted to talk to him about. The band was poised to release their second album when he quit.

"Sounds like a publicist's dream."

"Sure, but it was his worst nightmare." I didn't fill Cathy in on Boyd as secret agent, but I had a clear picture of why he might not want the limelight. "He dropped out of the music scene and changed his name and vanished. When Boyd died, everything he owned turned over to the crown."

"Was he related to the royal family?"

"No. It's called Bona Vacantia. In England, when there's no one to claim an estate, it becomes the property of the government. Boyd didn't have a family or a will. After the thirty year claim period, the crown donated it to charity, who took bids from competing auction houses. Harrington's Auction House won."

I thought back to the day Ronnie showed up at the *Ribbon Eagle* asking to buy the trunk and Monty encouraging me to take the deal. I thought about Ronnie's phone call before he drove into the tree, and I thought about what Petra's husband had said about her seeing a ghost.

I left the apartment building and walked to my car. My shoe connected with something small and round. I bent down and picked up a cufflink. It was a match to the one I'd found in the cigar box.

As I stared at the small object, I thought about my confrontation with Beatriz. I replayed my conversation with Vince and reconsidered the attitudes of Franny, Petra, and Phil.

I thought about the trunk reappearing at The Mod Holiday, the birth certificate hidden in the book, the spy gadget cufflink, the passports and recording masters and a hundred insignificant details that had added up along the way when I wasn't paying attention. I grabbed my keys and left. One person knew more than the others. It was time for another face to face.

———

DURING THE DAY, THE KIRKVILLE HOTEL LACKED THE atmosphere of danger and hostility from the other night. Cars and motorcycles were scattered through the parking lot at intervals, but no one loitered outside. I entered through the doors by the bar. Beatriz leaned against the wooden counter reading a book. There was one couple on the opposite side of the bar, and they were discussing the menu with a young male bartender.

Beatriz looked up from her book when I entered. "You came back," she said. "I didn't expect that."

"I didn't get to finish asking questions." I pulled out a bar stool and sat.

She closed her paperback and set it alongside the register. She grabbed a clean pilsner and filled with club soda, then set the glass in front of me.

There was a change in Beatriz's attitude. Less hostility, more weariness. The bruise on her cheek had faded to a dull greenish-yellow. Sunlight trickled into the bar from dirty windows and highlighted particles of dust that floated through the air by a highchair in the corner. I didn't ask what kind of person brought a baby to the bar. I didn't want to know.

"What have you figured out so far?" she asked. It was as if she knew me showing up again was inevitable.

"Boyd Brighton was a secret agent, wasn't he? He had half a dozen forms of identification and a couple of gadgets that belong in the International Spy Museum."

"Boyd was a government asset. I was his handler."

I'd suspected a lot of things over the past week but this wasn't one of them. "The rest of the world thinks he was a pop star."

"Being in The Modifiers was a cover that allowed him to move about the country with impunity. Doors open for pop stars, and we recruited Boyd to leverage that access. He'd gain information and report it back to me."

I was right! Boyd Brighton was a spy! I mean, stay focused, Samantha. "And who were you to Ronnie Holiday?"

She hadn't expected that question. Her shoulders tensed and her hands, already clutched together, turned white from lack of circulation.

"He was your son, wasn't he?"

She nodded and looked away.

"Who was Ronnie's father?" I asked gently.

"I got caught up in the lifestyle and made a mistake. The baby's father was the drummer for the band. He was a drug addict. Our cover was clean when it was me and Boyd, but when I got pregnant, everything got messy. The only way to protect the baby was to disappear. Boyd helped. He arranged for new ID and travel out of the UK. I had the baby and left two weeks later."

"You left the country with a two-week-old infant? Using government resources for your personal gain?"

She paused for a moment, and then continued with more confidence. "Once I left, I knew I could never come back. I'd been running Boyd's missions for a few years and I knew how to disappear. But when I got here, I knew my baby wouldn't have a life if I raised him while running. I did what I thought was right."

"What did you do?"

"I left him with a family in California, and I moved east. I sent them money to help with expenses. Last year I started getting phone calls. The man said, 'I know who you are. I know what you did.' Ronnie found me. I don't know how, but he did."

I understood how those phone calls would have shaken Beatriz up. Running from her past the way she had led to a life of always looking over her shoulder, and for what? She wasn't free. She was trapped in a prison of her making.

Beatriz aged ten years in seconds. Dark circles appeared under her eyes, and her eyelids drooped. The color drained from her face and her pronounced collar bone jutted out unattractively.

"Why were you so hostile to me?"

"It's been a long time since anyone brought up those days. I have a life here. The patrons at this bar are like family. But if they find out who I am, who I was, they'll never trust me again. Your questions threatened all of that."

"Is that why that big guy broke my phone and threatened me and my friend?"

"That guy is the owner. He served time in prison. The man you brought here was the cop who put him away. What happened the other night didn't have anything to do with you." She averted her eyes and I knew there was more. "Your friend, the one who did the mural at the mod shop. That didn't have anything to do with you either."

"He punched Eddie? Why?"

"There's a graffiti problem around Ribbon. When the owner saw someone painting the mod shop in the middle of the night, he got suspicious. He went over to investigate and found your friend —Eddie, you say?" I nodded, and she continued. "—asleep inside. At that point, he realized Eddie must have been hired to paint the store, but I guess Eddie woke up and took a swing at him. He hit back in self-defense." She picked up a coaster and tapped the edge on the bar surface. "He felt bad about that. He carried your friend outside and left him in his car."

Sometimes, it's interesting how pieces of information that appear to be connected are unrelated. And sometimes, seemingly unrelated things form a pattern. The toughest, most intimidating person I'd encountered since taking possession of the trunk was an ex-con restaurant owner who suspected *Eddie* of vandalism.

Go figure.

Beatriz leaned back and rested her arms on the table. "Well, then. You got what you came for."

"No, I haven't." This time the smile I gave her was genuine. "I was hoping you'd give me an exclusive."

"On one condition," she said. "I left everything behind when I left England. I barely remember who I was back then. It's silly, I know, but I'd like to see what else is in that trunk. Do you still have it?"

WHO KILLED RONNIE?

THE TRUNK. IT ALL CAME BACK TO THE TRUNK. I didn't still have it, but I knew where it was: at The Mod Holiday. The trunk still technically belonged to the newspaper. Any money paid by Ronnie had been extorted from Monty, so ownership was muddy. But it was after hours, and it seemed a whole lot easier to get into the store when Franny wasn't there.

"It's across the street," I said impulsively. I pulled out my set of keys to The Mod Holiday and dangled them.

Beatriz turned to the other bartender. "I'm taking a break," she said. He nodded, then went back to chatting with the patrons. "Let's go," she said to me.

There were two things bolstering my confidence. One was the can of mace in my pocket. The other was my plan to meet Loncar at The Mod Holiday after he dealt with his wife. If he wasn't at the store already, he would be soon. Beatriz was a hundred pounds wet, and I was pretty sure I could take her in a fight if it came to that. If I couldn't, I'd have to do some serious soul searching about my lack of fitness regime.

Everything Beatriz told me lined up to what I already knew. She had secrets that cast her in a poor light, sure, but she'd confessed to them. Would she have told me what she did if she were the one who killed Ronnie? I didn't know. But another thing nagged at me: the ease with which she told me her side of the story. It was as Eddie said when I first told him about the passports and the spy gadget cufflink. The intel was outdated; nobody cared.

We crossed the street from the Kirkville Hotel to The Mod Holiday on foot. It was late, and traffic was light. The storefront was dark. I fished Ronnie's keys out of my handbag and let us inside. The trunk was hidden under a blanket in Franny's office.

I dropped down to all fours and pulled the trunk out. The blanket fell by the wayside. I flipped the lid open.

Beatriz dropped down on her knees beside me. She pulled out a scarf. A plain white scarf with fringe along the end. For all of the colorful dresses, the derby shoes, the Chelsea boots and checkered tights and Bakelite jewelry, she reached for a simple white scarf. She pulled it out of the trunk and cradled it next to her cheek and closed her eyes.

"This was Boyd's," she said gently. "He swaddled Ronnie in it the night he was born. It's the one thing I always regretted not taking with me when I fled. If Ronnie had had one thing from those early days that he could have clung to, he might have grown up differently."

"Do you think it would have made a difference?" I asked.

Beatriz stared at the scarf. "Ronnie had fifty years of anger built up when he found me. I assumed he would have a better life than one I could provide while on the lam, but the couple told Ronnie who he was, and when he learned he was the son of someone from the Modifiers, he didn't let it go. He found out his dad died right around the time he was born, and he didn't accept that it was an accidental overdose."

"Was it?"

Beatriz hesitated for a moment too long. When she resumed her story, it wasn't with an answer to my question. "Ronnie ended up living on the streets. My hope was that he would have been raised in a stable house with the couple in California, but Ronnie picked up his father's habits. He was in and out of rehab by the time he turned fifteen. A girl from the clinic befriended him and asked her parents if he could stay with them until he turned eighteen."

"How do you know this?"

"I tried to keep in touch—not regularly, but when I could. They kept the truth from me for years. Everything I sent to help them care for him went into their pockets. Ronnie never saw a dime."

"I wasn't cut out to be a mother," Beatriz said. Her story had gone from a John Le Carré plot to a Shakespearean tragedy. She looked up at me with the white scarf clutched in her hand. "I abandoned my child, but I didn't kill him."

"You would have saved me a lot of effort if you did."

We both turned to the sound of an unexpected female voice. Franny Holiday stood in the doorway with a pistol trained on Beatriz.

WHAT MIGHT HAVE BEEN

"HANDS UP. BOTH OF YOU." FRANNY HOLIDAY gestured the barrel of the pistol at Beatriz and me. She was close enough that a trigger finger would result in Beatriz's death. "You probably already know you didn't clear the background check," Franny said to me.

"I had a feeling that might be a problem." I slowly raised my hands over my head.

"Stand up. Both of you. Leave the trunk."

Beatriz dropped the white scarf. I kept one arm in the air and used the other to grip the desk for leverage. After getting to my feet, I raised both hands again. "Out front. Both of you."

The three of us made a parade to the front of the mod store: me, then Beatriz, then Franny. Franny's pistol never wavered.

"Everything I could have had in life went to him. My opportunities were always cut short. 'What about Uncle Ronnie?'" she mimicked. "Everything I worked for was watered down by my mother's concern for a brother who wasn't even biologically related to her."

"You killed your uncle?"

"I killed Ronnie Holiday, but he wasn't my uncle. He was a lying, cheating blackmailer who stood between me and my future." She gestured around the interior the shop with her gun. "A mod shop in Ribbon. As if anybody cares."

I cared. Eddie cared. And I had the feeling, despite all of his flaws, that Ronnie Holiday had cared too. Then again, it's easy to make excuses for the dead. They're not around to tell you if you're right or wrong.

"Does your mother know?"

"I already told you she's on a cruise. Remember? My mother was blind when it came to Uncle Ronnie. I had to get her out of town so I could take care of him once and for all."

"Where did you get the cocaine?"

"It was his. I found it one day when I was going through his things." She sneered. "If I hadn't done it, he would have OD'd himself. That's who he was. His death was inevitable. I just gave Fate an assist."

"So the shop was just part of your plan?"

"Ronnie liked to talk about what might have been. I pretended I shared his interest in all things Mod and asked him questions whenever I could. He thought we were bonding." She laughed. "He told me his dad was a famous musician from the sixties. I didn't believe him, but then he mentioned the name of the band." She indicated the interior of the shop with the pistol. "That's how he explained this whole Mod thing. He said it was his legacy. I thought he was blowing smoke until he mentioned Boyd Brighton. I did some research, and do you know what I found?"

"What?" I asked. I already knew the answer, but I wanted to keep her talking.

"There's a record of an unnamed baby boy being born in Brighton, England on the day Ronnie claims is his birthday. Do you know what else I found out?"

I shook my head.

"The baby wasn't Ronnie. It was my dad."

She was so sure she was entitled to the estate of Boyd Brighton that I realized in an instant how I'd followed the wrong clue. "The unnamed baby boy from the birth certificate was your father?" I stared at Franny, and then looked at Beatriz. If Franny was telling the truth, then Beatriz was the grandmother she'd never met.

"You found it? The birth certificate?" Franny's eyes went wild. "Ronnie heard the stories from my parents, and when my dad died, Ronnie came up with a plan to get it all for himself. I knew he was an opportunistic bastard, but I couldn't do anything until I had proof. That birth certificate is proof. After my father died, everything should have been mine. Everything Boyd and the Modifiers created. The music rights, the masters. All of it."

"You killed Ronnie Holiday," I said. "You can't enjoy an inheritance from prison."

Franny had been motivated by an endgame that

justified her actions, and she never once considered she wasn't in the right.

"Ronnie wasn't my son?" Beatriz asked. She appeared to be as shocked by the news as I was.

"My dad wasn't your son either. You left him when he was two months old. You're nothing to me."

Franny raised her pistol and aimed at Beatriz. I reached into my jacket pocket and my fingers closed around the cufflink I'd found in Senior's parking lot. Franny shot Beatriz. Beatriz stumbled backward, into the fixture marked Birds, and then slid to the floor. "That was from your son," she said. She turned the gun on me. "This one's from me."

I raised the cufflink and pressed the stone as hard as I could. A dart flew out of it and whizzed past Franny's face. She was stunned enough to forget her impulse to shoot me. I pulled the pepper spray out of my other pocket and hit the plunger. A stream blossomed into the store. Franny put her hand up to her face and the gun fired. A bullet punctured Eddie's Mondrian-inspired mural.

As Franny stumbled around the store with her hands over her eyes, I charged. I put my head down and plowed into her, knocking her into the Blokes fixture. Hangers of Fred Perry polo shirts moved aside and we crashed into the center of the rounder. She dropped the gun and tried to claw at me, but I was too scrappy of a fighter for her to win.

"It's over," I said.

I called nine-one-one and reported the shooting.

By the time the paramedics arrived, Beatriz died.

Franny was led away in handcuffs.

The paper got the exclusive.

Kristi posted the story to our social media feeds, and it went viral. I had my fill of the limelight and gave credit to April May.

The recording masters buried in the bottom of the trunk contained a second Modifiers album. It was hard to establish a value for a piece of music by a band few people remembered, but it occurred to me that one particular collector might cherish it more than others. I arranged for the auction house to contact Vince on my behalf.

When all was said and done, I accessed the unboxing pictures Kristi took the very first day I opened the trunk. I blew them up and wrote the article I wanted to write all along: *Trunk Music: Notes from a Wardrobe by Samantha Kidd.*

Monty gave me the envelope of cash from his safe and I turned it over to Detective Loncar, whose deft investigative work provided more than I ever could have found out myself. I told him the money came with strings; I wanted him to train me.

EPILOGUE

I CONVINCED MONTY THE NEWSPAPER NEEDED A REAL
anniversary party. Kristi decorated the conference room
in paper flowers that matched her dress. Monty opened
a sixty-year old scotch and Frank volunteered to taste
test it. Carl lingered at his desk putting the finishing
touches on Ronnie Holiday's obituary.

The elevator doors pinged and two men in head to
toe black entered the newsroom` carrying white coolers.
This time, I expected them. The men went straight to
Carl's desk and opened fire—with silly string. By the
time they were done, Carl was covered in the stuff. José
pulled off his black knit face mask and Oswald pulled off
the other. "Gotcha, man," Oswald said. He handed Carl
a can and they came after me.

The party took place on the same day that Nick and
his dad were scheduled to return from Italy, and I left a
message inviting him to join us.

I was so deep into Eddie's debt that he got an

automatic invitation to anything I did, and today, he turned his back on the Whack-A-Mole graffiti game and joined me at the paper. While my coworkers mingled with local business owners, we hung out by my cubicle.

"Dude, you arranged for me to work for a murderer," he said.

"Technically, I arranged for you to work when the murderer wasn't there."

"Technically." He sipped champagne. "So, I had this idea." He set his cup down. "You know how your financial advisor is always telling you to invest in something more lucrative than shoes?"

"Yes."

"I was thinking. What if we bought the mod shop?"

"We?"

"You've got a bucket of money, and I've been contributing to a retirement plan since I was twenty. I'm a visual merchandiser, but I've spent the past week chasing a graffiti artist who contributed the most decorative illustrations I've seen in this town in a year." He took a sip of champagne. "Plus, the vandal was caught earlier today."

It was, as some might say, an example of mismanaged resources. The mayor of Ribbon had tasked the local police with the hunt for the graffiti artist, even prioritized it over the search for Ronnie Holiday's killer. Detective Loncar had advised me to let the cops come to me, but they never had. When things get personal, we tend to lose focus, and I guess there's no other way to take curse words on your sidewalk than personally.

"You *are* far more effective with paint than paint remover," I said.

"And you're a fashion retailer who uses a fake name to write articles that have nothing to do with fashion." He picked up his cup again, but he didn't take a drink.

I cocked my head to the side and considered his proposal. An unexpected side effect of this case was being back in that store, not just being there, but recognizing that I knew what to do with it. Franny had no interest in running a store. She wanted someone else's legacy to be handed to her. She'd wanted it to be easy.

I picked up my cup and clunked the plastic against Eddie's. "You're on," I said. "Let's go find Monty and start negotiating our lease."

By the time Nick arrived at the party, I was tipsy on champagne and excitement. I felt one chapter closing and another one starting and it felt good. It felt right. The air smelled of possibility and new beginnings, my favorite scent. (It was a little like cake.)

I greeted Nick with more than the usual enthusiasm. I didn't care that our home life was about to expand by a third now that I'd had senior evicted. I threw my arms around his neck and planted a kiss on his lips.

He returned the kiss with slightly less enthusiasm and disentangled my arms from around his neck. "Kidd. Hi. Wow. You're happy."

A secret agent might have compartmentalized the mission, but I couldn't wait to tell Nick all about it. Secrets were for the birds (and the blokes), but not for me.

I pulled Nick away from the crowd. "Did you get a lot done? Did your dad drive you nuts? How was Bardot? How was Blak Friiday? Are you going to collaborate? Before you answer, read this!" I handed him the newspaper. "I busted a spy ring! Let's never do this not-talking thing again. I've got so much to tell you!"

"I've got something to tell you too," he said. His voice sounded strained. He glanced behind him, and I followed his gaze. A five-year-old girl stood in the doorway with Nick's dad behind her.

The girl's curly brown hair was in ponytails secured with giant bows, and the print on her dress mimicked Murano glass windows. Her eyebrows were thick in the way adorable five-year-old girls can get away with, and her skin was sun-kissed as if she'd spent a week running around the Amalfi coast. Her tummy protruded against her dress and on her feet were the cutest little tweed Mary Janes I'd ever seen. She held the ear of a stuffed rabbit in one hand. The rabbit's feet dangled close to her knees. She looked directly at me, and I couldn't deny that I'd seen the exact same shade of her root-beer-barrel-colored eyes before.

Suddenly, telling Nick what I'd been up to for the past five days didn't seem important. My shoulders tensed with anxiety and my stomach flipped. The young girl studied me with the same intensity I studied her.

"Nick, who's the little girl with your dad?"

Nick turned to look at her and turned back to me. "Samantha, that's my," he paused as if the next word was a struggle. "Sister."

"Your *sister?*" Relief flooded me at the same time an arsenal of questions revealed themselves.

I looked over Nick's shoulder at the girl. Nick's dad was bent down, whispering something in her ear. She smiled. He pointed at me and when I looked into her eyes, I felt like I was looking into a very wise soul. Senior straightened up and smiled, equal parts bashful and boastful. An expression only a seventy-five-year-old man with a five-year-old daughter can pull off, I'd guess.

It's a good thing I'd cleared up the mystery of the trunk, because there was a whole lot here to unpack.

ACKNOWLEDGMENTS

Thank you to my readers and subscribers of the Weekly DiVa. Knowing you're waiting patiently for the next book helps motivate me more than a thousand deadlines!

Also:

To Amy Ross Jolly, for squeezing Samantha into your schedule. You are a treasure!

To Gigi Pandian, Ellen Byron, and Lisa Matthews. This book would not have been finished without your support and brainstorming. Writers are lucky to find a supportive team, and I've found one with you.

To Paul Weller and members of The Who, none of whom I know personally, for their unapologetic modness, which made the job of researching this book both fun and distracting.

To my other secret weapon: the retailers and creatives who keep the mod spirit alive through fashion choices, documentaries, and movies. (For a full list of mod resources I found while researching this book, click here: dianevallere.com/stark-raving-mod-resources)

To my close friends and family, who respected my need to shut them out while wrestling several ideas into a cohesive plot.

To Tom Sturgis Pretzels, for making sesame pretzel sticks.

And most importantly, to you. Yes, YOU! The person currently reading these acknowledgments! Thank you for embracing Samantha Kidd and her zany shenanigans. She'll be back before you know it.

XO,

Diane

ABOUT THE AUTHOR

National bestselling author Diane Vallere writes smart, funny, and fashionable character-based mysteries. After two decades working for a top luxury retailer, she traded fashion accessories for accessories to murder. A past president of Sisters in Crime, Diane started her own detective agency at age ten and has maintained a passion for shoes, clues, and clothes ever since. Find out more at dianevallere.com.

Want a bonus ebook that you can't get anywhere else? Join the Weekly DiVa Club and receive BONBONS FOR YOUR BRAIN, a collection of humorous essays about everything from writing mysteries to buying shoes to being the best version of yourself. Get the offer at dianevallere.com/weekly-diva.

The Pajama Frame

Lover Come Hack

Apprehend Me No Flowers

Teacher's Threat

The Kill of it All

Sylvia Stryker Outer Space Mysteries

Fly Me To The Moon

I'm Your Venus

Saturn Night Fever

Spiders from Mars

Material Witness Mysteries

Suede to Rest

Crushed Velvet

Silk Stalkings

Costume Shop Mystery Series

A Disguise to Die For

Masking for Trouble

Dressed to Confess

Made in United States
North Haven, CT
04 July 2023

38552144R00161